Short Stories for the Christian Life

SHORT STORIES FOR THE CHRISTIAN LIFE

Ralph D. Curtin

RESOURCE *Publications* · Eugene, Oregon

Resource Publications
An Imprint of Wipf and Stock Publishers
199 W. 8th Ave., Suite 3
Eugene, OR 97401

www.wipfandstock.com

PAPERBACK ISBN: 979-8-3852-2651-1
HARDCOVER ISBN: 979-8-3852-2652-8
EBOOK ISBN: 979-8-3852-2653-5

VERSION NUMBER 10/10/24

DEDICATION

The Christian Life is comprised of trials and triumphs, both designed to bring glory to God. His Holy Spirit grants us the power and grace that enables and empowers us to endure and overcome trials that lead to never-ending triumphs.

These short stories are about those who experience trial and triumph in today's world as well as the near future.

Many thanks to my helpmate, Kathy, in the preparation of this work.

CONTENTS

FAMILY

FOR BETTER OR FOR WORSE

I n a quiet town in Long Island, New York, the cool September breezes flowed through my car windows as I cruised home from work. The year was 1969. As I turned into the driveway I gave a quick wave and nodded to my wife as she waited at the door. With three busy toddlers, it was unusual for Kathy to stand vigil, except on rare occasions like birthdays, anniversaries, or tragedies. Knowing this, an ominous feeling enveloped me.

"What's the matter Kathy?" I asked as I walked in the front door. "You and the kids okay?"

Looking to release the tension in her heart, she blurted out the news: "Randy, it's your mother. She's in the hospital. Your father called an hour ago—but I wanted to wait until you got home—they brought her in an ambulance, something about a drug overdose. . . "

". . .Overdose?!" I broke in with disbelief. "Oh no." I reached for the nearest wall to hold me up and added, "Damn pills. Damn doctors. How's my dad?"

"Sounded upset, but controlled," she replied with concern. "He said she was unconscious; her stomach's been pumped. They're still working on her. You had better leave as soon as possible. I made you a sandwich to eat in the car."

"Right." I answered as I unraveled my tie and threw it on my bed just as my five-year-old trooped in from the backyard.

"Hi Dad! How's your day going? Tough huh?" he said brightly.

Concealing the crisis, I answered with a forced smile, "Not too bad; how's my boy?"

3

"Fine." he said gleefully, then added with a puzzled look, "Will grand-ma be alright?"

I glanced at his mother and said, "Lord knows. . . I'm sure. . . prob-ably. . ." The staccato reply came from my wondering all the time how astute and observant my son was for his age.

* * *

The parkway traffic began to ease as the sun faded over the horizon. The repetition of the tires striking the pavement joints faded into a muffled cadence as I turned to deep thought, thought about mom and the past. Although there were some bright spots in the dreary backdrop of my adolescence; my youth was primarily troubled. Mom's indulgent behavior, along with a below-normal income household, painted a scenario that could only bring problems. In fact, there would be no release of anxiety until I married and moved out of the house. I was then independent; Mom couldn't shame or hurt me anymore with her foolish acts.

One event in particular really left a deep scar. It occurred at a party I held at our home one Friday night in 1961. Dad was out on a sales call and after an hour, mom made a scene. My friends were very embarrassed for me. We were all dancing the "slop" to Dion's music when mom came out and did her version: an Indian war dance, complete with cosmetic war paint. It was apparent she had been drinking and taking drugs, despite her pre-arranged promise to me.

* * *

I arrived at the hospital, the same hospital that brought two of my children into the world. At the reception desk, the nurse courteously answered my inquiry, "Your mother is on the second floor, in the hallway, Mr. Conner. We're waiting for an available room."

I was relatively stable until I saw my dad, then I broke down inside. I looked down at the inert form on the portable bed, then asked my dad about mom's condition. "Too soon. Too soon," he lamented as he shook his head.

I scanned his weary face, then embraced him and asked, "What did the doctors say?"

"They pumped her stomach, mostly tranquilizers, could go either way; fifty-fifty," he said in despair. He reached for her limp hand, began stroking while remembering his marriage vows in a whisper, ". . .for better or for worse. . .for better or for worse. . ."

I probed impatiently, "Dad, I know you're upset, but how did this happen? Was it deliberate?"

Trying to maintain his composure was difficult and within seconds he yielded under the strain of the situation. "I'm strong physically, but it's hard for me to refuse her," he whimpered. "I always let her take her own medication, then she loses count. On purpose? I don't know. What with the wine and the prescriptions, I guess she went too far. . ." His voice faded as he closed his eyes in anguish.

A surge of anger came over me. I thought, *how could you allow this to happen? What kind of relationship would foster this indulgence and utter disregard for self-control?* I couldn't help but become terribly saddened. A once beautiful woman, who at one time appeared to be in love with life was now reduced to an obese drug-addict. *From wine to pills to the morgue,* I thought. Permissive doctors, pharmacists, and unfortunately, a permissive husband, unwittingly contributing to the ruination of a loving, determined woman. *What a gruesome scene,* I thought.

The all-night vigil proved fruitful. Mom stirred, gave us a look of resolve, then turned over to sleep off the effect of the drugs.

The doctor examined mom, then spoke to me privately and said, "Your mother is very strong-willed. I expect she'll pull out of this; it appears her drug tolerance is very high. She'll have to be watched of course. Then there's the law," he added.

"The law?" I asked.

"Yes, New York law mandates a psychiatric examination in every case of attempted suicide. She'll be remanded to a mental hospital for evaluation. It's for her protection. If indeed there is an abuse here, it can be treated and before long your mother could be well again. We're talking heavy drugs here." He looked down at his clipboard and rattled them off, "Thorazine, Elavil and Valium. Together they work against each other and produce serious effects. Obesity, continuous diarrhea, gastrointestinal disorders—a vicious circle," he concluded while shaking his head in reproof. He then walked away.

Dad looked broken. Broken by bizarre happenstance and beaten by the callous weather of life. A man humble in spirit, reaching out for help like a stranded swimmer unable to rescue himself. "What did he say?" he asked, hoping I would sort out the pertinent data.

"Mom will be alright. Probably in several hours she'll come around," I said while verbally amending the doctor's report. "The doctor recommends therapy. Just until she's feeling better. A place where the staff is more equipped to deal with her condition. The hospital is close by, in Central Islip."

"Central Islip!" he cried out. "That place is for psychos and retards. . . not for your mother. I couldn't put her in there."

I assured him the doctors were making the right decision and we must trust them. We then agreed to stand watch in shifts; Dad then departed to rest while I stayed with Mom. For me, the night was interminable. There were frequent groans and once a loud wailing where Mom called out for God to help her. Then for His forgiveness. Then for Dad's. Later on the body rocking, eye rolling and vomiting took it's pound of flesh. After two days in the hospital, the time came for Dad to bring Mom to the mental facility. The day I dreaded. The day I'll never forget.

My home phone rang and Dad said, "Randy I couldn't do it," the nervous voice said. "I escorted the ambulance to Central Islip. I saw the compound . . . the people wandering; the matrons—I just couldn't—" He gulped for air, then added, "you wouldn't believe how things are there! When I first checked your mother in, two orderlies that looked like armed guards rushed her off to some upstairs room. Then I heard screaming and carrying-on coming out from behind the metal door. It was awful. Then your mother shrieked and yelled out, 'HELP ME JOHN! DON'T LEAVE ME HERE IN THIS SNAKE PIT!' So I signed her out. . ."

I sympathized and consoled him as best as I could, even though I believed the account was exaggerated. I asked what his plan was and he said that a psychotherapist would see her regularly. In addition he affirmed that he would dole out any medication, sit with her during withdrawals, and act as her male nurse to see her through. I stifled my tears, then wished him God's richest blessing, adding that I would be out within a few days to look in on them.

When I did, my heart was thrilled to see that Mom was really trying to get by without her drugs.

* * *

Thirteen years have passed, and just last week I got a call from Dad asking me to come out to help him pick Mom off the floor of the living room to put her into bed. She had lost count of the pills she had taken, got dizzy and fell.

She didn't get hurt this time.

PLEADING THE FIFTH

J im Hinkley woke up earlier than usual when he realized it was Father's Day. For him and his wife, Nancy, it was not a joyous holiday, but a day of sorrow. There was ongoing angst between them and their two children, Andy, age 21, and Shirly, age 20. *Why is this so?* he thought. *What did we do to deserve this continuing trend in society for the youth and millennials to disown their parents when they didn't agree with their philosophy or their lifestyles?* He didn't understand the dilemma but he did remember a famous preacher saying the acid test of a father's leadership was the condition of his home. *Am I to blame?*

He knew in his heart that he did all that God's Spirit had directed him when it came to being the example of a godly parent, knowing that God's structure for humanity was first, the government, second, the church, and finally, the family. For him, he knew he demonstrated this by showing his kids that he, along with them, should live according to biblical standards which included a special love for their mother. So what was going on? He also remembered Pope John Paul saying, 'the future of the church and humanity depend on the family . . . the family is the measure of the greatness of a nation,' and J. E. Hoover saying, 'that high crime rated is traceable to the disintegration of family life.' More importantly to him was God's decree with His Fifth Commandment, *Honor your father and your mother, that your days may be long upon the land which the Lord your God is giving you. Does that apply to today's standards and lifestyles?* He was perplexed.

"Happy Father's Day!" Nancy said as she entered the kitchen where Jim was sitting at the table enjoying his biscotti and coffee. "I have a special card for you," she said as she poured herself a cup of tea. Jim nodded as a flashing reminder in his mind of the past Mother's Day came upon him where he showed their children—their teenagers—that his wife was someone special and treated as one who deserves special treatment in their marriage and from their children. But they were nonchalant and detached from the family holiday designed to bring respect to the parent. They simply observed the family day for their mother with a greeting card that lacked any personal note of respect or recognition.

"Thanks, I needed this," Jim replied with a smile after reading the card that reflected his wife's words of her approval of him. Then he picked up his cell phone to check on any Emails or messages. There were none.

"Any texts or Emails from Andy or Shirley?" They were both out of their state with their friends celebrating their college break for the summer. Jim felt their break went well beyond the norm since they were repeatedly gone for more than six weeks each year.

Jim shook his head. "Not yet," he replied optimistically. "I'm sure I'll hear from them soon."

Nancy, real casual, laid back. Her thoughts of the current trend for children to disown their parents began to seep through her thinking process. She postulated: "Well, hopefully they will recognize today as a special day and let you know how important you are to them."

"From your lips to God's ears," he replied trenchantly then took another bite of his biscotti then another slug of his coffee. *Then he waited.*

By dinner time it was apparent there would be no recognition of his fatherhood by their son or daughter. *No Email, text message, or phone call. Nothing.* He was upset and greatly disappointed. Being soul mates after many years of marriage, Nancy realized he needed to talk to somebody beside herself who could minister to him. "I think we should go and talk to pastor Warren about our view of how our world has changed and that as parents we can use an explanation. Prayerfully he can help us."

"Okay with me. I need some spiritual, godly advice," he replied, his voice vibrating with intensity.

* * *

Calvary Christian church, with its four pastors and two thousand members, decidedly went against the Christian Left movement that threatened their view of God's plan of salvation and the lifestyle of a believer on Jesus

Christ. Pastor Warren believed in the literal interpretation of the Bible along with its literal fulfillment that extended to the future view of the apostasy that was plaguing the corporate church. Both Jim and Nancy valued Calvary's doctrinal position and supported it as their home church. Seeking counsel from pastor Warren came easy to them as they believed he would give them godly advice supported by biblical texts.

Pastor Warren waved to them from his office doorway as they waited to see him. "I received your text message, Joe," pastor Warren said as he nodded to Nancy and added to her, "nice to see you again as well." He warmly ushered them into his office and motioned for them to sit in the two upholstered chairs facing his desk. Known for his frugality, his office displayed modest furnishings and wall decorations while his bookshelves were adorned with hundreds of books covering every level of theological commentaries from conservative Christian authors as well as several versions of the Bible.

"Welcome Jim and Nancy," Pastor Warren began while hugging them both. "What brings you here this morning?" His persona was genuine. They sensed his role as a pastor was really a calling from God, not just a career. "Coffee?"

"That would be nice. Black, no sugar or cream," Jim said as Nancy waved him off.

Pastor Warren complied. "Problems?" he asked while pouring the coffee.

"Pastor, we need an ear to help us process what we see going on today. The image the bible portrays is that the family provides a message of hope. The family is the unit through which God perpetuates his covenant so God's family will be known.

"So many families are estranged and hurting today—ours being one of them. Now I know that the bible teaches that in the end times there will be a great falling away from bible principles and certainly the Word of God prophesied the great apostasy that will proceed Christ's return, but our hearts are searching for a way to reach these victims and provide some godly advice and hope."

Nancy raised her hand with a broad smile. "Let's start with our family. In the honesty of the Word of God, we fear that our children—now teens— are unsaved, and worse . . . " she began to say dolefully, " . . . think they are, but in our minds, are make-believers. The outworking of this is that they have written us off. It seems to me that the Fifth Commandment of 'honoring your father and mother,' has been erased and certainly forgotten.

"The younger generation has developed their own doctrines of right and wrong and have decided if you want to be a part of their lives, you will accept their points of view or they simply reject you and your advice." She paused and glanced at her husband.

"Pastor, Joe added, "what we are troubled about is that we cannot reason out how did we get this far away from God's holy Word, full of instructions on how to have your family enjoy abundant lives? Don't misunderstand us, we are not referring to an easy life. On the contrary, the Word tells us we will have tribulation in the world but be of good cheer, Jesus has overcome the world."

"When did the world and the corporate family stop wanting Jesus?" Nancy added while swallowing hard. "We know the Christian life is not easy and we can't do it alone. We need godly friends and neighbors to encourage each other—to help each other—to care!"

Pastor Warren was well experienced in the field of listening. To hear the entire issue be it a complaint or a praise, he would employ his ears before employing his mouth. "Go on," he said while pointing to Joe.

"Do you think the focus changed when we started to have two income families; not necessarily because of needs but of wants?" Joe began dryly. "Make no mistake, it's tough getting kids up and dressed for school, then breakfast, working a full-time job, picking the kids up from after school care. Then we have to get dinner on the table and help with homework along with a bath and getting the children ready for bed. Something has to suffer with a schedule like that. Pastor, I think we both know what gets put to the side and our culture and society reflect that."

"Is it any wonder that our children have been spoon fed by the Internet which is a weapon parents don't seem to recognize," Nancy noted while sighing deeply. "We sit here pleading the fifth—not the rule of law—but the Fifth Commandment. There is no codicil saying if the parents meet their expectations or whether in their minds you were good parents. How did our priorities take such a shift? It seems we all live according to our own personal agenda. Over the past three decades the American conscience has been given anesthesia by many sources. Among them is our social media, liberal college professors who teach evolution and humanism as if it is fact. Even the church has lost its power and voice."

They both paused in their quest in seeking godly advice from their pastor.

Pastor Warren remained silent momentarily while tapping lightly on his desk. He was thinking. He remembered reading about the Fifth Amendment that in the United States Constitution it guaranteed that an individual cannot be compelled by the government to provide incriminating information about themselves in what has become known as 'remaining silent by taking the Fifth.' When the individual 'takes the fifth' they invoke the right to refuse to answer questions or provide information that might incriminate them. But both Jim and Nancy were pleading the observance of the Fifth Commandment that in his mind carried a weighty penalty if disobeyed. He recalled the passage in Deuteronomy twenty-seven that said, 'cursed is the one who treats his father or his mother with contempt.'

"Jim, I wish your story was original, however, over the years I have heard similar expressions of grief. We live in perilous days where right is wrong and wrong is right," Pastor Warren began. "Maybe it's time this church gets serious about praying and believing God. So many in this congregation have prodigals. Let's pray them home! I'll announce at Sunday services that we will hold a weekly prayer meeting expecting our Lord to answer the deepest requests of our hearts.

"I know that Satan is working diligently to divide the family," Pastor Warren added as a muscle jerked in his left cheek. "You can see his handiwork in the media, especially when it comes to sitcoms like *Bevis and Butthead* where fathers are portrayed as buffoons or *All in the Family* where Archie is viewed as a numbskull incapable of making a worthy decision without help from the younger generation. These situation comedies give credence to the current trend of the younger generations to abuse their parents as well as their grandparents."

He stood up and walked to his bookcase and added as he pointed to his prophetic book section, "The Bible predicted in Second Timothy the current trend that would preclude Christ's Second Coming where children would abuse their parents in spite of a godly upbringing that would include ungratefulness, disrespect, and if that weren't enough, turning them over to authorities if they were not compliant with the national abandonment of God."

"How did we get here?" Nancy asked impulsively as she shook her head as if hearing a doomsday message.

God uses our difficulties to develop our character, Pastor Warren thought as he realized this applied to the world, America, the corporate church, and the family. Difficulties were abounding everywhere to bring the world to cry out for Jesus to fix things since man's methods were failing miserably. "We got here one small step at a time," Pastor Warren replied. "Over the past four decades society's political, biblical, and moral values have dramatically diminished to the place where we accept these violations as normal. If they had come about rapidly, I believe the church would have recognized this and would have attempted to thwart this invasion before it was accepted as a modernization of our value system."

He walked back to his desk and then pulled out a business card from a drawer. "In view of your situation, I am going to recommend you visit with a colleague of mine who is an excellent Christian counselor. His name is Dr. Michael Stein. I don't profess to know all the answers, but while we as a church will pray as we discussed, I think you both would benefit from his advice."

Jim rose to take the card as his shoulders rose and fell. "Thanks pastor for your guidance," he said joyfully. "We will contact him."

"Remember this," pastor Warren said in conclusion. "Suffering is not meaningless, suffering is temporary, and suffering is measured."

* * *

Jim smiled at Nancy after pulling into the Stein counseling agency parking lot and pointed to the sign that read: *Renewed Hope Christian Counseling.* "Positive and hopeful," he said.

"From your lips to heaven," she agreed immediately.

Once inside the office the modest middle-aged receptionist handed Jim a clipboard and said cheerfully, "Welcome! Please complete these forms and the fee application before your visit with Dr. Stein."

Jim handed the questionnaire to Nancy. "You know how I hate paperwork."

Nancy blinked in torpid agreement and proceeded to complete the forms. Fifteen minutes later a young couple exited Dr. Stein's office whereupon the young man said to Jim, "This guy is good!" and then the couple waved to the receptionist and left the building.

At first glance, Jim thought Dr. Stein reminded him of who he conjured up in his mind that the apostle Paul would look like. He was about 50ish, small in height, bald with a black and gray goatee, and slightly rotund. Surprisingly, in the mind of Jim, the office lacked a gaudy appearance which in his mind was a good thing since he was here to seek godly wisdom, not to be impressed with the décor.

"Welcome my friends," he began, pointing to the small sofa in front of his desk. "Have a seat and tell me how can I help you."

Nancy glanced at the wall behind his desk that proclaimed his degrees that included his Doctor of Ministry in Biblical Counseling. Next to the wall of his fame was a painting of a Mogen David embossed with a crucifix with the title Yeshua, the Messiah—the fulfillment of all messianic prophecy. She was truly impressed that he was a Jewish man who received Christ as his Messiah. She was elated.

"As you probably know that pastor Warren referred us to you," Jim began, "in hopes that you can give us some advice and direction on how to deal with our two college kids who stay detached from us."

"Not only 'detached,' "Nancy added forcefully, "but deliberately hostile when it comes to our advice and outreach to bring harmony back into our family."

Silence.

There was a stillness in the room as if Dr. Stein was processing the complaint. Nancy recognized the thought process where he was asking for divine guidance from God's Spirit before answering.

"What you may perceive as rebellion in your family is actually a fulfillment of bible prophecy where our culture encourages insurgency against authority—including parents—as a so-called *right* in light of the 'me generation' where the population is only concerned with 'self.' From a biblical perspective the Levitical law makes it clear that parents deserve respect without earning it—"

"That's it!" Nancy shouted as the shock rippled through her. "You called it!"

"The Word of God makes it clear," Dr. Stein continued, "that the divinely orchestrated family cannot be replaced. The family was established before the church as the basic human organization. No other structure can replace the family. The family is the central social context of human life and is the chief means of God's communication with human beings. The enemy is determined to destroy the family by introducing such things as bedroom TVs, cell phones, and other instruments that promote independence from the family unit. Our present society is the outworking of his handiwork."

"Is the corporate church to blame?" Jim asked innocently.

"I don't believe the church is solely to blame, but there is the problem that plagues the church that is whether the churchgoer is a follower or a true believer since apostasy is rampant in these last days. In other words, the unsaved Christian is being persuaded that by going to church they will wind up in heaven. The outworking of this philosophy is that we have a great percentage of church members who think they're regenerated Christians when indeed, they are not. This in turn effects their view of the government, their church, and of course, their parents." He paused then opened up his Bible and turned to the gospel of Luke.

"Listen to this word of prophecy by Jesus," he said with authority. "'Do you suppose that I came to give peace on earth? I tell you, not at all, but rather division. For from now on five in one house will be divided: three against two, and two against three. Father will be divided against son and son against father, mother against daughter and daughter against mother' . . . " he paused then finalized his reading: " . . . this prophecy is being fulfilled in your ears today."

Jim kneaded his temples. "In my understanding of the biblical mandates, as you said, we as parents deserve respect without earning it, so in our case, we have certainly lived lives commensurate with the bible's view of godly parents, so why is this happening to us and to many others in the church?" His words were fraught with tension, he needed answers.

"In our world today, and this includes the church, we see the violation of the Fifth Commandment—no question about it. But then, again," he soothed, "there is a penalty that accompanies those who violate the Fifth. Not sure this will help but God's Word maintains that to those who participate in this way of life that dishonor their parents, their life is shortened, they are cursed and will experience repercussions that in today's vernacular is 'what goes around comes around.' In other words, your two children—unless there is a reversal of their attitudes and treatment to you both—will be treated the same way by their children."

Nancy harrumphed. "I remember reading in Exodus where children who disrespected their parents were executed so as to set an example to those other children in the ancient tribes so they would not imitate them."

"Nancy, please!" Jim said while shaking his head. Then he turned to Dr. Stein. "Nancy is just venting. You can see how disturbed we are over this whole thing."

"Dr. Stein," Nancy asked wearily, "do you believe that we are being held ransom? In other words, either we capitulate and approve of their treatment of us and knuckle under to their viewpoints or they will hold our future grandchildren as hostage until we cave in?"

Dr. Stein snuffled then stiffened. "Unfortunately, I do see this trend increasing in our country as well as the church." In order for him to put a positive spin on their session he added, "Remember, the Lord is in control of all things as Paul reminds us in Romans Eight and we need to keep our eyes on Him until either our family is healed, or the problem is solved in society, or Jesus comes back to take us to heaven."

"Until then, what should we do?" Jim asked with his eyes slightly blurred by tears.

"Keep in touch with them until they close the door," Dr. Stein proffered. "Take the first step, don't wait for them to initiate contact. Treat them as prodigals and continue to reach out."

That was confirmation for Jim. 'Treat them as prodigals' was basically what pastor Warren said. *Yes, that will be our approach,* he reasoned, knowing Nancy would follow in his thinking. He reminded himself, the Lord does not always take us *out* of difficulty; many times he takes us *through* it.

Dr. Stein ended the session in prayer.

Both Jim and Nancy thanked God for the counsel. It really helped them.

* * *

Pastor Warren looked at the recent worship service attendance numbers and was delighted to see a moderate increase. *As promised, prayer is working.* Praising God would follow.

He remembered his conversation with Jim where they agreed they would petition the throne room of God to bring about change in the church that included remedying the detachment between parents and their kids. It had been a while since he met with him. He had to call him. "How did your session with Dr. Stein go?" he probed over the phone.

Recognizing their close relationship, Jim rejoiced in the call from his pastor. "Both Nancy and I were refreshed in the spirit after our counseling session," Joe said blissfully. "We were not only refreshed, but relieved when he reminded us that God is in control and that we are to continue to pray our prodigals in."

"That's good news," Pastor Warren replied softly and confidently.

Jim could sense his pastor's relief over the phone. "Thanks for your prayers and concern for us," he replied. "I heard the Lord is answering our prayer in the church—" he stopped and then said, "—now that's good news as well."

"See you on Sunday," Pastor Warren returned gleefully.

* * *

Three weeks later as Jim drove home from the church budget meeting his cell phone rang. "Dad, this is Andy, we need to talk."

CRYING OUT TO GOD

T rinity University located in central Florida boasted of many assets to develop a better way of life for those seeking to follow and learn more about God. The weather was semi-tropical with plenty of sunshine, the Christian theology was conservative, the tuition was reasonable while offering credited Bachelors, Masters, and Doctorate degrees. The school's emphasis was on preparing men and women for both pastoral and educational ministry.

For Dr. Itzak Cohen, TU was more than just a job as a professor of Biblical Studies. It was an opportunity for him to tender to God's sheep and offer any counsel or guidance to the flock under his tutelage. After six months under his teaching, Joshua Morris trusted him and believed he could ask him for advice.

He was very troubled in his spirit about his family.

Joshua had great respect for Dr. Cohen who taught at TU for three decades and possessed an uncanny ability to defend God's Word when any one of his students would challenge his position on Biblical truth. Be it Creation verses Evolution or the different aspects of eschatology—the study of end times, he was able and willing to go head-to-head with any contender who offered alternatives that did not align with the Bible.

It was after a Friday morning class that Joshua decided to ask his professor for guidance after listening to him teach on the inspiration and inerrancy of Scripture. If what he said was true, then he could depend on him to give godly counsel that would help in solving his family dilemma and its far-reaching effects.

It was a little more than ten minutes after Dr. Cohen closed the session in prayer before Joshua could approach him. Due to his uncompromising teaching and popularity, several students lingered about to seek clarification or hear his personal interpretation of the issues he raised during the class time.

"What's up, Josh?" Dr. Cohen asked with a smile, recognizing the perplexed expression on his face. Together with his current lack of classroom participation and overdue assignments it was apparent there was a problem considering his zeal in the class over the past three years. Once again, he would offer his counsel should the need be made known.

Dr. Cohen was a little pudgy with a goatee and a receding hairline but was also known as 'Mr. Dress-up' because he was the only full-time professor who wore a sports jacket, a shirt with a Christian tie, along with designer jeans. Yes, to many he was odd, but sought after for his congenial Christian manner that showed in the way he loved his students.

"Is it possible to talk to you over a cup of coffee?" Joshua asked Dr. Cohen in a hopeful manner.

"No problem. Love to talk," Dr. Cohen said smiling luminously then picked up his attaché case and led the way to the cafeteria.

Once on the serving line, Joshua pointed to a piece of cherry pie in the display case as Dr. Cohen gave him the nod. "One for me as well," he said. At the register Joshua paid the tab with his money from his part time job as a waiter in a neighborhood fast-food takeout restaurant.

"I can sense that you're troubled," Dr. Cohen began while leading the way to a secluded spot in the cafeteria. "What seems to be the problem?"

Joshua took a sip of his coffee then began to emotionally fill up as tears began to form in his eyes. "I have a family problem that is worsening and getting the best of me. The problem is affecting my whole life, especially my ability to concentrate on my studies. I've been having a difficult time sleeping—sometimes crying during the night—and the bottom line is that I'm questioning God and am not able to clarify my future. I really need help."

Clasping his hand, Dr. Cohen soothed, "Now take it easy and let's talk about this."

His voice had a calming effect on Joshua. He nodded several times then took a bite of his pie. After several seconds he took a deep breath and said pensively, "My parents—who claim to be believers—are talking about getting a divorce due to what they call 'incompatibility' and I believe my younger sister is into drugs and leaning toward the LGBTQ movement—"

he paused and squeezed his eyes shut. "I don't know how much more I can handle! I know as Christians we shouldn't be anxious, but I'm having a tough time managing all this.

"I remember reading that Luther said that 'a true believer will crucify the question, 'Why,' he will obey without question.' But for me, I realize that David wrote in the messianic Psalm twenty-two that Christ cried out from the cross on Calvary: 'My God, my God, *why* has thou forsaken me?' So I believe I can do the same. Lord, *why* have your brought all these problems into my life and my family?"

Dr. Cohen took a slug of his coffee after swallowing a spoonful of his pie then gently placed his coffee cup on the table and said, "Joshua, having problems—be they spiritual, emotional, moral, financial, or otherwise, is normal for anyone living in our world today. This extends to both Christians and non-Christians." He patted his hand and added, "But for Christians who are obliged by God's Spirit to handle their problems in a godly fashion—differently than the nonbeliever—there is a proven method that is designed to work. In short," he added with a tight smile, "we have the Bible to guide us, give us hope, and relieve us of the pressure of life by replacing that pressure with the joy of the Lord. Unfortunately, the unbeliever is deprived of this blessing and attempt to solve their problems by other means. Many of those means end in disaster.

"From my perspective, when we receive the Lord, his Spirit through the Bible shows us how to manage difficulties such as family issues, health problems, career paths, in such a way to avoid having a 'pity party.' Evidence of a close relationship with the Lord brings us to that place where we stop questioning his providence since his ways are higher than our ways."

"That includes complaining, right?" Joshua said impulsively.

Dr. Cohen grinned expansively. "That's right—as hard as that is to avoid."

"I'm not there yet," Joshua said, his tone conveying disbelief.

"Not that I want to air my dirty laundry but—" he paused to shake his head, "—but allow me to share an episode out of my life with you so that you understand that you're not alone when it comes to problems and complaints," Dr. Cohen advised after taking a deep breath.

Joshua nodded his support. "Well, if it's okay with you, it's okay with me. My lips will be sealed."

"Good," Dr. Cohen replied then went into his instruction mode. "You'll remember when we were studying the Old Testament that the will of God was often revealed through the Urim and Thummim that the high priest would employ to respond to a question that was often asked of him by the ruling king in a difficult situation, especially when it came to military matters. The Urim and Thummim consisted of three gemstones that were kept on the high priest's ephod—his holy garments—and one would illuminate when a question was asked. I often liken them to a modern-day traffic light. I think one was red, indicating a 'no' from God, one was yellow, possibly indicating a 'not-now' response, and one was green, meaning a 'yes' or go forward from the Lord.

"I bring this up because we don't have the Urim and Thummim any longer—it was never seen after the destruction of the Temple by the Babylonians, but we do have another form of determining God's will that is much better—it's the Holy Spirit and the Word of God!"

"Now that was really cool!" Joshua remarked as his countenance began to brighten.

"Today we have other resources to help us in addition to God's Spirit, and his Word," Dr. Cohen continued. "We have our pastors, our parents, our prayer partners, and our own spirit-filled conscience to guide us into determining God's will.

"So in my own case, I recently went through a battle in my heart that was developing here at the college. There were some trustees who were hinting that we were too conservative and old fashioned—not being open to adjust our doctrines and our teacher's teaching methods that included our theology and were urging the dean to 'modernize' our school to conform to the majority of colleges to attract the favor of the—" he paused, "—what I call the liberals and the Christian Left. They also hinted that it would enhance our chances of getting outside funding."

Joshua was shaken. "So what did you do?"

Dr. Cohen stiffened then replied, "I did what I'm urging you to do. I went into God's word." With that he pulled out his thumb-indexed bible from his attaché case and opened it to Psalm 77. Joshua looked at the worn cover, the dog-eared pages, the handwritten notes, and the red lines with arrows pointing to key words on the document. It was a sign to him that this man not only was diligent in his studies, but that his bible was his manual for life.

Feeling obliged to follow along, Joshua pulled out his cell phone and opened up the Bible app to the same text. Dr. Cohen gave him an approving nod then began. "Here's how the psalmist, probably David's musician, related to me. In the first six verses he cries out to God in a sense of pleading because he was troubled—much like you are today. His soul refused to be comforted like a sick man refusing food that would nourish him. Then he complains as if to say, 'God what's happening?' He adds in this passage that he's so troubled he can't sleep nor can he speak or pray—" he paused then added, " . . . sound familiar?"

Joshua just sat quiet and blinked several times as he began to digest this counsel.

"He continues to voice his reason for crying by adding that he sought refuge in the past and how his God helped the patriarchs so why not me? He's worried and makes diligent search of his past life with God. He begins to examine his life. But before he allows God's spirit to help him climb out of the pit he's in, he argues with himself and begins to go from distress to despair. Then he asks God six questions: Have you cast me off? Will you not be favorable to me again? Has your kindness ceased? Have your promises ceased forever? Has my God forgotten to be gracious? Has your anger shut up your tender mercies?

"This is the descent into the cavity of despair where this attitude impacts the spirit, then the heart, then the mind, then the soul, and finally the body." He fixed his eyes on Joshua with a penetrating stare. "You don't want this."

Joshua had to be engaged. "So what does the psalmist do? What should I do?"

"The remedy is right here," he said, patting the page on his bible. "Listen to the steps of delight that enable you to climb out of the pit. Remember Paul's exhortation in Galatians Six, 'Let us not grow weary while doing good, for in due season we shall reap if we do not lose heart.' In other words, you can't give up—you must press on.

"So the psalmist forces himself to press on by saying, '*I will* remember the years of God's mercy. *I will* remember the works of the Lord. *I will* meditate on his works since his ways and deeds are good. He summarizes by saying, 'Who is so great a God as our God?'"

Joshua shot him a look then asked, "So how did you apply this to your problem with TU? Did you apply these principles to your life?"

"I didn't at first," Dr. Cohen admitted sheepishly. "I needed further instruction to confirm what the psalmist promised—" he stopped and then bit his upper lip and added, "I know what you're thinking. If my professor asks for further confirmation from God's word then where does that leave me? Right?"

Joshua rolled his eyes. "You're into mindreading too?"

"I dug deeper into the '*I wills* in the bible for confirmation," he advised. "But before I did that I remembered one of my colleagues reminding me of God's promises where he says that any suffering from God—be it spiritual, emotional or physical—is not meaningless, it is temporary and that it is measured—"

Joshua suddenly set his iPhone to notes and wrote in the three promises. Then with eyes pleading for understanding asked, "Then what?"

"I discovered another set of '*I Wills*' in another psalm that spoke to my heart with confirmation because it was an answer to my pledges from God." He turned to Psalm 91 and added, "The Lord responds to the psalmist by saying, 'because he has set his love upon me *I will deliver him; I will set him on high* because he has known my name. He shall call upon me and *I will answer him; I will be with him in trouble; I will deliver him and honor him. With long life I will satisfy him* and show him my salvation.

"This settled the problem in my mind because this was a response from God to me because this set of '*I Wills*' is directed to the psalmist—or the believer—from God himself. After we do *our wills*, God does *his wills*. The promises remind us of our need to depend on the Lord. This entire exercise of faith has set a standard for my life."

Joshua looked at him inquiringly, contemplating his next question. "With that dose of wisdom, you then left the problem at the foot of the cross for God to handle. Right?" Joshua asked.

"Hmm, yes," Dr. Cohen said then gave him a thumb-up. "God's answer and inner voice to me was that I should approach the dean and explain my concerns and as long as my theology and spiritual convictions were not going to be compromised, I should stay on," he explained. "This was to be God's will for me."

"So what happened?"

"I believe out of my longevity of service and my testimony—and somewhat popularity with the student body—that the dean called in the rest of the faculty to hear their side of some of the changes he contemplated making," Dr. Cohen postulated. "The rest of the faculty body were not in favor of his moving to a more liberal curriculum so he tabled the move until another time."

"So you won!" Joshua said.

Dr. Cohen's shoulders rose and fell. "At this time, yes. But in my mind I see the impact our liberal society has had on Christian ethics and unless there is a Holy Spirit revival, the Christian colleges will cave in to the demands of the secular world. Then, for me, it will be time to move elsewhere." Then he took a deep breath and asked hesitantly, "Where does my sharing and counsel leave you?"

"I'm going to go home and sit down with my parents and sister and have a show down!" he replied, his voice vibrating with intensity. "They have to agree to do things God's way or no way."

"My only concern now, Joshua, is that you allow God's spirit to lead, guide, and direct you. You don't want to bulldoze or attack them with your new-found spiritual application," Dr. Cohen advised soothingly. "You want to give them time to 'process' your counsel and then come to a decision—that you hope—will be pleasing to the Lord. Right?"

"I guess you're right, Dr. Cohen," Joshua added as an afterthought. Then he signaled his professor who counseled him with a wave that he was leaving, shook the tab in the air, and added, "this was a small fee to pay for such a vast amount of wisdom." Then he exited the cafeteria and drove home.

* * *

Conditions in his household were no different now that three days had passed since he met with his professor, Joshua realized. But in his heart, he needed three days to digest the guidance and lower his anguish that accompanied his thinking of meeting with his family. *The enemy thrives in conflict*, he thought, but then again, he remembered that Jesus said, 'I have overcome the world.' He had to face the challenge in the power of the Holy Spirit. That he knew.

Waking early in the morning with great expectations Joshua walked into the kitchen, made a pot of coffee then proceeded to toast an English muffin that he would then coat with peanut butter and jelly. His favorite breakfast food. Fifteen minutes later, his sister, Allison walked in, stilled dressed in her pajamas.

"Good morning Allison," he said cheerfully. "How's things with you?"

"I'm cool," she replied with a derisive snort. "How's things with you?"

He knew in his heart that he needed to take a gentle approach with his sister in order to penetrate her defensive mechanisms the world taught her.

"I'm doing well," he replied softly. "Any chance you have a few minutes for me to share some thoughts with you?"

"Yeah, that'll work. What's up?" she chirped.

"Allison, I hope you know how much I love my little sister. If I haven't been there for you I regret that. It seems our family operates on our own daily agenda and we have lost the fellowship and unity we once enjoyed.

"The world has such a perverted view of life as our culture is filled with loose morals, drug abuse, and acid rock music which sows seeds of violence and mistreatment. I want to be here for you, sis. I want you to know you can talk to me about anything, come to me for advice or we can just spend some time together as brother and sister."

He took a slug of his coffee then began dolefully, "We both know what's going on with mom and dad. So I've been asking God for advice on how to deal with it—"

"Me too," she inserted. "So what's your plan?"

"I spoke to one of my professors confidentially about mom and dad because I'm really upset about what's going on here at home. I view my prof as one who has wisdom and to make this brief, he really helped me. I came to realize that God uses difficulties and trouble to reveal how deep the word of God has gone in our lives. So, he urged me to read God's word—the Bible—and to approach them in love to appeal to them from God's perspective."

Allison squinted at him and said, "Now that's heavy!" Then she gave him a look and began to hum the theme from *The Twilight Zone*.

Joshua patted the air then said, "I need to ask you where you stand with God because that will tell me where to go next in our family situation."

"Well, I know there's been family conflict and I don't want to see mom and dad divorce, that's for sure," she replied. "As far as I'm concerned, I'm good with God. I mean we're tight."

"You're good with Jesus as well? You decided to receive him as your Savior?"

"I've been thinking about it since I've been watching your life, bro," she replied with a grin. "And, truth be known, I'm cleaning up my act."

It was reassuring to him that his testimony and life mirrored his relationship with Christ but he still had a long way to go. "Thank you for that," he replied.

Silence.

He had to leave the rest with God and let his Spirit handle her steps to salvation and regeneration. If she's working on making a commitment to God, that's good. That in itself was an answer to his prayer. He suddenly remembered the bible text Dr. Cohen reviewed with him out of Psalms. *Yes, the 'I wills,'* he thought. For his part, he had to remember the text where the Lord promised to provide all his needs according to his riches and glory. *That was good as well.*

When Joshua stood up to fetch his second cup of coffee, his dad suddenly walked into the kitchen, helped himself to a cup as well, then said with a tear-filled expression, "Your mother and I talked through most of the night and decided that we would seek Christian counsel and keep working on our marriage relationship. I don't know if it will help. We have many differences and opposite ways of handling difficulties. However, I am keeping in mind your mantra, *Is anything too hard for the Lord?*"

"Dad, I'm delighted to hear about this decision about Christian counseling and I'm sure the counselor will ask the both of you to remember why you fell in love in the first place. But nothing takes the place of the word of God. When did you and mom stop opening your bibles together? Have you and mom stopped praying together?"

"Son," he began slightly muddled, "I can see how our troubles have affected you and for that I'm sorry. Even parents can get so involved with their own feelings where they fail to recognize what's happening around them. Rest assured that your mom and I are committed to do the work that leads to reconciliation."

A wave of happiness washed over his face. "Thanks dad. Allison and I want you to know that we are here for both of you."

Smiles permeated the kitchen as mom walked into the room. She took an assessment of the atmosphere and the emotions that were flowing and said, "What's going on here?"

Their dad grabbed their mom and gestured to his two kids and said, "We need a group hug! The Holy Spirit has reminded me that there is nothing more important than family—after Jesus of course."

Joshua was so overwhelmed with the grace and mercy of God and the blessing of answered prayer that he could only cry out to God in his heart the praise, *Hallelujah!*

THE RENEGADE

B ay Cove, Florida, located twenty miles south of downtown Jacksonville, provided Donna Westcott many advantages for a middle-aged
woman. She believed she was a good wife as well as a good mother, and
with her master's degree in accounting she could work at a prestigious
firm that offered rapid advancement, excellent health benefits, regular in-
creases in pay, and still keep everything in balance. These advantages were
good enough for her to want to stay working until her old age benefits
kicked in. *Or so she thought.*

Her salary together with her husband Paul's, a mechanical engineer
for Aerodyne, a local aerospace manufacturer, enabled them to easily afford
a four-bedroom home in a luxurious development like Bay Cove. And then
there was their only child, Brandon, age 15, who, in Donna's mind was a
conundrum, wrapped up in an enigma, inside a mystery. Someone she just
couldn't figure out. But then again, she didn't have the time needed to do so.
Until something happened that would change everything in their household.

"I'm leaving for work now, Brandon! Do good in school!" Donna
yelled from the landing on the staircase to the second level of their home.
Being fully dressed in her suit and heels she glanced in the mirror at the
foot of the stairs and said to herself, *We got this!*

"Okay mom will do! Be safe!" he yelled back. Moments later he heard
the double car garage door opener cranking, her Mercedes starting up, seconds past, then the garage door closing. Then he went to his bed and raised
the mattress and then stuffed the hidden sandwich bag into his backpack.
Then he closed up the house and rode his eBike to the Bay Cove high school.

* * *

Chamberland Inc. is a very prestigious accounting firm with nationwide locations, their Jacksonville office being the main hub. Featuring corporate tax attorneys, accountants, and offices in local strip mall stores provided them with the title of America's financial tax wizards. Donna was proud to be a part of it all. But this vocation had its price: a major strain on the husband-and-wife relationship. The spirit of professional and financial competition was taking its toll in their home that would only lead to a family disaster. Brandon often witnessed the escalating conflict between his parents in their home but he didn't know how to fix it, so he found consolation by other means.

"Mrs. Wescott," Donna heard over the office intercom from the company's switchboard operator, "you have a call on 01 from your son's school counselor."

Donna swallowed hard then picked up the phone. "Yes, this is Donna Wescott. Is my son alright? Is there something wrong?"

"Mrs. Wescott," the counselor replied awkwardly, "this is Mary Kelly the counselor from the Bay Cove High School. I'm afraid things are not alright. Mr. O'Donnell, the school principal, asked me to call you directly since he believes this is a family problem and wanted you to act on this problem in the home."

"Well, what is the problem?" she asked, mystified.

"Our janitor found your son smoking marijuana in the boys bathroom and reported it to the principle. Then there's the issue of his behavior where he is disruptive in his classes and he doesn't do his homework that is reflected in his low grades. As a result, the principal has suspended him." She paused, then added, "The principal wants you to come to the school and pick him up."

His mother started to wretch her guts. "Um, I'm thirty minutes away so what will happen until I get there?"

"I'll keep him in my office until you arrive," the counselor replied. Seconds later she asked, "What about his father? Is he closer? Can he pick him up?"

That's the one thing I don't want until I know what's going on with him, Donna thought. "He's further away. No, I'll be there as soon as possible. Please keep him in your office," she replied apologetically.

* * *

"We will speak to your father about your suspension after he's had his dinner," Donna said in front of the kitchen oven as she prepared to broil the sirloin steak. *My mother always said you should address any family problem after everybody's stomach was filled.* She would follow her advice today.

Brandon shrugged his shoulders and gave his mother a snide look. "Whatever."

The minute Paul walked into the kitchen from work and saw the table set with the steak ready to be cooked on top of the stove, and Brandon standing in front of the sink tapping his foot on the floor, he knew something was up. Something bad. "What's going on? Everything okay?"

Donna walked to him and gave him a big hug and a kiss on his cheek. "We'll talk about it after dinner. In the meantime, tell us how's things are going at Aerodyne while I cook the steak and potatoes."

Paul glanced at Brandon suspiciously with his arms crossed over his chest. "Things at Aerodyne are same as usual," he replied warily. "Should I be worried about home?"

"Nothing we can't handle," Donna replied then handed him a glass of his favorite wine.

The tension in the room was palpable for the first five minutes, until the wine began to slow Paul's rising anxiety. "Any good mail?" he asked after finishing the first glass then refilling it.

"Just junk," Donna answered then placed all the food in the middle of the table after throwing the advertisement mail in the trash can.

"It's nice to have you share dinner with us tonight, Brandon," his father said in a somber tone as his son sat at the table. Ordinarily Brandon ate his dinner in front of the TV by himself while his parents ate in the kitchen. Part of the disassociation movement captivating families.

"Learning to flow with the masses," Brandon replied with a dismissive wave of his hand.

His father traded looks with his mother as if he was trying to read the scene unfolding before him. He forced a smile at his wife and asked, "How's everything at your office?"

"Same as usual."

Paul realized they were communicating in short sentences and the dialog was not very flowery. Without finishing his vegetables and setting aside his chocolate cake and coffee he turned to Donna and asked, "Okay, what's the problem?"

Donna sipped her tea and then nodded toward Brandon. "Our son was suspended from school today for possession of marijuana. I had to go to the school and pick him up and hear the rhetoric from his counselor about how bad his behavior and grades are." She starred at him impassively and added, "He's a mess and we need to do something about it!"

Paul slammed his fist down on the table. "This is what happens when we let him do—" he paused and made quotation marks in the air, "—'his own thing' and don't keep watch over him."

Donna's read between the lines. "Oh, I get it!" she exclaimed rhetorically. "It's because I'm working to pay half our bills on this house and not staying home babysitting!"

Paul gave his son a venomous look and grabbed hold of his hand in an effort to deflect Donna's complaint. He squeezed it and said, "Tell me what happened!"

"No big deal," he replied flippantly. "The custodian was told by some nerdy dude that I was smoking some weed in the boy's room. So he reported it to the principle who then handed me over to the school counselor." He smirked and added, "So they did some checking and saw that I'm—" he paused to circle his forehead with his hand in a mocking fashion and continued, "—I'm not the brain that you and mom are so they suspended me."

"You didn't add that your teacher complained that you're disruptive in class, you don't do your homework, you are failing her quizzes, and what she told me later is that you're a bad example to the rest of the class," his mother noted.

"This is all the outworking of the new mentality that is 'me and self,'" his father said vehemently. "And as far as your mother and I are concerned, we worked very hard to get our degrees so we could get good jobs so we could keep you in a good neighborhood, a good school, good clothes, and pay for your eleven-hundred-dollar eBike!" His father then gave him a lethal glance then asked, "How long is the suspension?"

Brandon hesitated fractionally. "Three weeks."

"You stay put!" his father breathed pointing to his place at the table. "We'll be right back!" Paul motioned to Donna and said, "Let's have a sidebar." She nodded and accompanied him to their adjoining dining room. "I'm thinking that he needs to experience another family's situation to give him some contrast so that he realizes how good things really are around here and that he's a fortunate son.

"I want you to talk some sense into him and if he listens and agrees to change his ways, then we'll work with him," he proffered. "But if not—" he paused and shook his head, "—then I want to send him for the time of his suspension to my brother's house so he can see what the other side of the family is like."

Donna liked the idea but needed assurances. "Tommy and Patty will be okay with this? And what if he returns and there's no change?"

"I'll work this out with my brother. It will be fine. What happens if there's no change, well we'll deal with that as it comes," he said.

"Okay. I'll talk to him," she replied. The love a mother has for her son had to be recognized while the love that a father has for his daughter was to be recognized as well. "You go to school to pick up his eBike then come home and take your shower."

The wine took its effect. "Got it," he conceded.

Donna went back into the kitchen.

* * *

"So what's the deal?" Brandon snapped the moment she returned to the kitchen. "Am I to be sentenced to prison? To solitary confinement?"

Donna pulled out a chair at the kitchen table and sat down across from him then replied bristly, "What no, 'I'm sorry'? No 'I'm sorry I upset you, mom'?"

A muscled jerked in his left cheek. Very sarcastic: "Whatever."

His mother stiffened. "Oh really? 'Whatever'? Well we're tired of your rebellious attitude."

"Oh, yeah, well I'm going to run away," he replied.

"And then what?" his mother asked. "You're only fifteen years old. Will you get a job to support yourself? Where will you live? How will you eat?"

"I don't know yet, but I'm sick of the house and school rules and restrictions," he added.

"Seriously? You're sick of being a part of our family? I don't think you comprehend what that means. To be a part of, you participate, you don't just take, you also give. That includes jobs such as mowing the lawn, putting your dirty clothes in the hamper and placing your dirty dishes in the dishwasher. You live like your father and I are your servants, with the express purpose of making you happy," his mother argued.

"That's not true! But I don't like the nagging and the pressure to do my homework and get good grades. I don't need that and besides I plan to quit school when I turn sixteen."

"And then what?" she repeated with heightening volume. "Your father and I encourage you to excel and prepare for your future. A future that brings you satisfaction of a job well done. Everyone needs a purpose in life and some of the decisions you make now will reflect on your future—" she broke off and pointed at him and added, "—choices Brandon have consequences both good and bad!"

Brandon looked straight at his mother and said, "I don't believe you."

"Well okay then, you leave us no choice," she argued. "What you might not understand is that your father and I are legally responsible for you until you're eighteen. Since we are not the parents you want, we are going to have you live with your uncle Tommy for a while."

"AND THEN WHAT?" he shouted.

"Well maybe your uncle Tommy and aunt Patty can reach you where we have failed," his mother replied softly to counter his attitude.

He got a wounded look on his face. "And then what? You forget that I'm your son?"

"We could never do that. Your father and I will always love you," she continued. "Listen to me. I have worked my whole life to create a sanctuary, a place of peace and comfort and camaraderie for my family but you have rejected your father and me. This may come as a shock to you but this is our house and our rules. We don't answer to you and we will not let your terrible attitude affect our family."

Brandon saluted his mother. "What if I decide not to go? And then what?"

"You don't have a choice in this matter," his mother insisted. "Either you admit you are wrong in your thinking and actions or you will be forced to leave. But if your agree to the house rules and we see a change in your ways, we will sit down and go over why you changed your mind and what that means."

"And then what? So either I knuckle under and accept the house rules or I get out right?" he questioned bitterly.

"Look, Brandon," she appealed, "we want to guide you towards a future of hope and a belief system that promises the abundant life. It's that simple."

"You mean your idea of an abundant life. And then what? Still there would be your rules, right?"

"Absolutely, so think carefully about your decision because you will have to live with it," she summarized then stood up from the table and placed her hands on her hips. "You have until your father returns with your eBike to decide." Then she walked out of the kitchen.

He shook his head. *I know my uncle Tommy doesn't believe in all these rules. I need to get out of here.*

* * *

Donna met Paul in their garage as he unloaded Brandon's eBike from his SUV. After hitting the button to lower the garage door, she walked to him and said, "Bandon and I had a little chat while you were gone and I don't see any remorse or willingness to change."

Paul nodded and said gruffly, "I figured as much so I called my brother on the way home and ran the situation by him and he's all in. He'll help where and when needed."

"Patty is okay with this?" she asked, knowing that any disruption in a family's lifestyle can bring unwanted problems.

"She was there when he picked up his cell phone and he gave her a brief synopsis and she gave him a thumb up," he replied optimistically.

Donna bit her lower lip. "Okay, are you going to take the next move or do you want me to?"

A thought flashed through his mind. *I know what she's thinking. I spend too much time at work and on my time off I play golf with my buddies so there's no time to set an example in leadership at home so she must take charge.* He suddenly recognized his responsibility. "No I'll talk to him."

Donna nodded as they both headed for the kitchen.

* * *

"Did you get my bike?" Brandon asked his father as he walked into the kitchen. He was enjoying a peanut butter and jelly sandwich he managed to make for himself during the interim. The steak his mother made for dinner was unsuitable to him.

"Forget about your bike!" his father replied fiercely. "Your mother gave me a summary of your little talk and apparently there is no change of heart and no plan to change your ways," he added sternly. "If there was a change, that would mean that you stay home which is 'option A.' So we're going with 'option B.' So pack your things tonight because tomorrow I'm bringing you to uncle Tommy's house."

Brandon slammed his hand down on the counter, "FINE!" he shouted and began swearing at his father.

Paul exchanged hostile glances with Donna then jumped in front of Brandon and raised his fist in a threatening manner. "PAUL!" Donna yelled. "Don't—!"

Paul pointed to the doorway and flared, "Get out of our sight!"

"I can't wait 'til I get out of here!" Brandon mumbled to himself and sheepishly walked out of the kitchen then thought, *I won't have to take any*—he used a profane word—*from them!*

* * *

It was Saturday and Brandon was surprised that his father took time off from work to drive him to uncle Tommy's house. A six-day work week was normal for his father. To pay him back for this outrage, he didn't say a word even though he suspected his father's fury had subsided. He could see his demeanor was greatly relaxed. *Who cares?* he thought. *They don't care about me! When I get to uncle Tommy's I can do what I want.*

When they arrived at uncle Tommy's house, Paul was delighted his brother's construction company's truck was still there. He needed to solidify a few things face-to-face. Moments later Tommy walked out to greet them. "Take your suitcase and books into the house while I talk to your uncle Tommy," his father commanded the moment he turned off the ignition.

No answer. Just a scowl.

"It sounded over the phone that you have your hands full with him," Tommy said after giving his brother a big fraternal hug.

Paul hesitated fractionally. "Donna and I are hoping you, Patty, and your boys can talk and put some sense into him. Otherwise—" he paused and shook his head. "—not sure where to go."

Just as they reached the front door, "We'll give it our best shot."

"Where are your boys?" Paul asked once inside the house. Surprised.

"They're out working. On the weekends they work with me on my jobs. I just came home because you were coming here with Brandon," Tommy explained.

"Hi Paul," Patty said as she gave him a hug. "Cup of coffee?" she asked pointing upstairs. "Brandon's getting settled."

"No. I have to get to my office to finish up some stuff," he replied.

Patty sighed. "Give Donna our love. Tell her I'll call her later."

"Will do," Paul replied and shrugged in a self-depreciating way and left the house for his office.

Moments after Paul left, Tommy pointed up the stairs and said to Patty, "I'm going to speak to Brandon and set down some ground rules before our boys come home. Pray for me." *Destruction must give way to construction,* he thought.

Patty nodded then clasped her hands together in a prayer-like fashion. "Will do."

When Tommy opened up the door of the bedroom Brandon would share with Freddy, their oldest at age seventeen, he was sitting on his bed listening to something on his cell phone through his AirPods. "We need to talk," his uncle said loud enough to overpower his cell phone.

Brandon bristled. "Okay uncle Tommy," he said and set his phone down then removed the AirPods.

Paul sat down next to him on the bed and softly tapped Brandon's knee. "As your uncle I want you to know that we are all family. Your parents only want what's best for you so they asked your aunt and I to pitch in and help you to settle the conflict in your house," he began. "But in order to help, you will have to agree to what we do around here," he paused then nodded, "are we good so far?"

Brandon harrumphed. "I guess."

"To begin with, we are a church-going family so you will be expected to go with us to church while you're here," he said as he ticked off the items with his fingers. "Next, we are a working family where your cousins work with me on Saturday's and on their days off from school so they can learn a trade, earn some money, get some good exercise, and work together as father and sons."

"Um, I had no idea—" Brandon gulped. "—do I have a choice?"

"No," his uncle replied firmly. "Your dad is my brother, but we have different standards and different approaches to family life—especially in view of current social principles. But I love your father as well as your mother but ultimately we have to account to God for the way we do things. For your aunt Patty and I, we want the Lord to bless us so we do things his way," he explained.

Brandon's nervous system clicked on as if an unseen hand had thrown a full-power switch. "I don't know if I can handle all that," he grumbled nervously.

"No choice!" his uncle replied. Then he stood up from the bed and laid out the itinerary: "Get settled. I will pick up your cousins who are out working and then we will have dinner. Lights out at 10:30 tonight, and up early at 7:30 tomorrow for church. Got it?"

"I guess," he repeated. He had no advance report, knowledge, or idea that he would be leaving a home to get freedom and then to become a slave.

"Oh, and one more thing," he added rigidly. "You'll be working with me starting Monday while your cousins are in school. Breakfast at 7:30 and we leave for work at 8:00 A.M. Wear your jeans and be ready to get some good exercise." Then he walked out of the room.

Brandon's heart jumped. "Ugh!" he muttered.

* * *

When Paul returned from his office, Donna immediately asked him how things went leaving Brandon at his brother Tommy's house. "I didn't stay as I had things to clear up at the office."

"What? You didn't stay and help Brandon get settled? You didn't talk to Tommy and Patty and tell them how grateful we for their help? They probably think we just wanted to dump our problem on them, not to mention what Bandon must think," Donna replied.

"Oh, right," he argued. "Once again you could have done a better job. If you had all the right answers, our boy would not be in this situation to begin with so don't go there, Donna. I might work late but you bring your work home."

"Let's not do this, Paul," Donna pleaded. "It is easy to judge and blame but it doesn't offer a solution. We need to sit down and explore where we stopped looking out for each other and making time for each other. Is it any wonder why Brandon shows out the way he does? Maybe he is looking for some affirmation that he is important to us and that he is loved by us. Since we haven't shown much of that to each other, let us agree we have not set the example we intended."

Paul escaped to a moment of contemplation. "Maybe we have been so focused on our careers and justify the long hours without admitting that somehow joy has eluded us—" he paused for further thought, then: "—my brother Tommy and his family love and serve God. Do you think that is where we missed out? Perhaps our hearts would be more connected if we loved and served the Lord. You have to admit something is definitely missing in our lives and Brandon seems to be the resultant factor."

Donna nodded as if in agreement. "I guess we should be asking ourselves are we willing to make a course correction and how much that change would look like."

"First things first," Paul replied. "Tomorrow is Sunday and we will go to church and ask the Lord for guidance."

* * *

REDEEMER CHRISTIAN CHURCH

After being welcomed by the pastor and listening to his sermon on priorities and how often they get skewed, Paul felt a nudging in his conscience about his family. He had to have a serious talk with his wife. "I'll treat you to lunch at Tid Bits," he said as they drove out of the church parking lot. "You good?"

Donna looked perplexed but smiled and said, "I'm good."

While waiting for their tuna melt sandwiches they ordered, Paul turned to Donna and asked, "What is the most important thing in life to you?"

"Funny you should ask," she replied curiously. "I've been thinking of that the whole time the pastor was speaking and I remember my first goal was always to be a good wife and mother. I have really wandered from that goal and focused on what I thought made me happy but never has."

"Okay," Paul said. "Thanks for being honest. Now I will try to do the same. I always felt you were smarter than me and that if I could provide the luxuries of home and cars and the country club you would respect and love me more."

Teardrops fell from Donna's eyes as she listened to Paul. "I never wanted those things but because you were brought up so poor I thought they were important to you, but all I wanted was you!"

Paul began to tear up as well. "I guess we both have been living a lie. You are everything to me, Donna, and I love you very much!"

"And I love you as well," Donna said as she reached across the table and clutched his hands.

"Now we have some readjusting to do," Paul pledged.

"Yes, we certainly do," Donna agreed.

* * *

Lasagna happened to be the Tommy and Patty's favorite dinner, embellished with toasted Italian bread with a fluffy green salad and cherry tomatoes. Their sons would rather have macaroni and cheese or hamburgers on the grill with a side of fries. But tonight they would do something different. Tommy brought in a variety of subs from a local Subway, not really knowing what Brandon liked. It was Patty's way of welcoming him and not being occupied with the menu so she might participate in the conversation more fully.

"Good to see you again, bro," Freddy said to Brandon the minute he walked in with his brothers. Freddy was their lanky seventeen-year-old with long brown hair in a ponytail but his brothers were more like their dad. Mike, at sixteen and Rodney at fourteen were both slightly chunky due to their propensity for sweets, something their mom specialized in. Blueberry cupcakes, chocolate chip cookies, and cherry pie being their favorites.

Patty referred to her kitchen as her 'domain,' where no family member dared to mess with. But it was also like her office. She would listen to the Christian oldies while occasionally humming to one of her favorite hymns, sometimes remembering the lyrics, but most of the time she would concentrate on family matters while baking and asking God for wisdom to aid her husband in leading the family.

Tommy said grace at the dinner table then his firstborn Freddy pointed to Brandon and said with a smile, " Dad told us you would be staying with us for a while. That's really cool!"

"Yeah," Mike added, "I hear you're really good at video games."

Rodney chimed in. "And you can help us with doing our yard work."

"Plus we get paid for working with dad. Besides our allowance that is," Freddy added.

Brandon simply shrugged his shoulders and waited for the signal that it was time to start eating. *Whatever*, he thought.

"Okay guys let's dig in," Tommy announced.

Everyone noticed that Brandon asked no questions and replied to others in two syllable words, none of which were interesting.

After dinner they all gathered in the TV sunroom and watched CBN for several minutes to catch up on the news then they watched a G-rated 50s movie converted to Blu-Ray.

Brandon was bored to death. He retired to his room early and by the time Freddy arrived he was fast asleep.

* * *

BAY COVE CHRISTIAN CHURCH

Brandon was advised of the Sunday schedule by Freddy on the way to church and for a moment he thought he might enjoy going to the teen ministry and seeing how what he called 'The Bible Thumpers' live and act, but he was predisposed to believe the worship service that followed would give him a cramp. *But what he didn't know about is that God had a plan for him.*

The size of the congregation of Bay Cove Christian numbered somewhere between twenty-five hundred to twenty-seven hundred and had a mixed age group from seniors to millennials, to teens, to expectant mothers, to newly-weds. The exact number was unknown since many were transients, dead, or moved to other churches. It would be a novel experience for Brandon.

Brandon followed Freddy into the teen ministry classroom on the second floor of the education building while Freddy's brothers were assigned to the lower floor. He estimated that there were like twenty other teens, both boys and girls, mulling around, poking fun at each other, while some were just sitting in the rear of the room reading their bible. "How long is this class?" Brandon asked Freddy the moment he walked in.

"One hour. Then we go into the sanctuary for worship service," Freddy replied then poked him in the chest and asked, "We're good?"

"I guess," he replied woefully.

Moments later the teen pastor walked in the room. He was in his 30s and wore jeans with a tee shirt and sandals. He took a quick visual survey then walked over to Freddy. "Who's this?" he asked nodding to Brandon.

"Pastor Bruce, this is my cousin Brandon," Freddy replied then put his arm around Brandon's neck. "Here for the first time so make it a good one!" he teased.

"We'll try," pastor Bruce said and walked to the front of the classroom.

"Let's sit in the back," Brandon suggested as he waddled toward the rear of the classroom passing by four girls who were chatting away, teasingly mocking each other.

Graciously accommodating him, Freddy followed then quickly grabbed his cousin's hand stopping him short in the middle of the aisle. Then he pulled one of the chairs with his other hand next to one of the girls. Then he said to her as he patted Brandon's shoulder, "This is my cousin Brandon. He's staying with us for a while." Then he pointed to the girl and said, "This is Kathy. She's one of our stellar performers."

At first Brandon just nodded then an instant later he said, "Hi. How 'ya doin'"

"Seriously?" Kathy said then added, "I like a man of few words."

Brandon took his seat then stared at Kathy for several minutes, observing her, taking inventory of her features, her manner of speaking, noticing her interaction with the other girls. Something in him changed. He couldn't explain it.

"Okay! Okay!" Pastor Bruce shouted. "Let's take our seats and open our Bible's to Luke chapter fifteen. Seconds later as the chaos subsided he said, "Let's go to prayer first." Then he pointed to Freddy. "Freddy, open us up with prayer and don't forget to mention Israel, our government, our church, and our families."

Freddy bowed his head thinking, *That's a lot to pray for.*

But he prayed masterfully, receiving a nudge and a thumb up from both pastor Bruce and Kathy.

Pastor Bruce divided the Bible text into three sections then called upon three students to read aloud the parable of the Prodigal Son. "Good read," he announced admirably. "Now let's look a little closer at this and make some application for us today.

"First, the son represents a sinner like every one of us. This son apparently wants to be on his own because he is tired of the restraints at home, his ordinary daily chores, and is enamored by the world's attractions. So he asks his father for his inheritance—we can liken this to one of you asking for what you believe you're entitled to—and his father then gives him what he wants because his father recognizes that his son really desires to throw off any restraints and that only God can change him.

"Next, we interpret the text to show that the son decides to indulge in reckless, immoral behavior to give him the 'fix' the world offers. He is really enjoying himself—" Pastor Bruce paused to look at the class, "—or so he thinks, until God's purposeful trials begin to afflict him. He becomes destitute and is forced to feed pigs and live among them, which according to Levitical law is considered an abomination—a lesson to us that sometimes the things we desire turn out to be a curse.

"The world's system and attractions begin to disappoint him and suddenly he comes to his senses. Now for us, we believe when this begins to happen, it's the Holy Spirit opening our eyes to the truth and calling us to God, so our prodigal begins to recognize his sinful attitude and behavior and confesses his insolence to God—he repents of his sins. Then he realizes that things back home were really not so bad. So he begins his journey from the faraway land that represents the world's system only to find that his father saw his coming and ran to greet him. When he met his father he cried out for his forgiveness who kissed and embraced him as a sign that at one time he was considered to be dead but was now alive. Then they celebrated his return with a huge party. This is God's message for us today." He closed his Bible and said, "Now for our remaining time talk among yourselves and see where this fits in your life."

Freddy turned to Brandon who looked confused. "What did you think?" Freddy recognized his cousin's lack of interest in pastor Bruce's message. To him it was a sign that he was still in unbelief.

"I think it's a stupid story," Brandon replied sourly. "If someone really did that, his father wouldn't give him a party. Do you people always talk about sin? It's boring man!"

Brandon shrugged his shoulders then scanned the room.

Freddy noticed his cousin fixating on Kathy so he waved to her to join them in a corner. *Could this be a 'God-thing'?* Freddy wondered. He winked and nodded at Kathy and said, "I have my car here, so what do you say we go for pizza after church?"

"Love to," she replied while smiling at Brandon.

* * *

Brandon took a long visual survey of the church sanctuary when he first entered. Once he was seated in the pew his cousin Freddy said the pew was 'theirs.' Before the worship service began he explained what he meant. "Our family always sits in the same pew every week as if it was assigned to us and our name was on it."

"Oh," Brandon said then continued to scan the sanctuary, impressed with its lack of luster and grandeur. He noticed that behind the choir's row of chairs were two flags, one the American, the other, Christian, with three floral arrangements between them.

Once pastor Eddie stood behind the pulpit he complemented the worship ministry on their ability to bring the congregation before the Throne Room in preparation to hear God's Word. Then he opened his Bible and said as he turned on his soothing voice, "Today we will explore God's view of rebellion." From there he turned to various texts then highlighted the subject with ample insight he used as ammunition to support his view. He explained: rebellion seems like freedom but has limitations. There is no greater rebellion than not to believe God's promises. Sin is rebellion against God. The essence of sin is rebellion against divine authority. Then he summarized with this statement: to convert one sinner from rebellion will cost God crucifixion.

Oh, here we go again, thought Brandon. *These people are nuts.* But the congregation was mesmerized.

Freddy nudged Brandon during the altar call and whispered, "What did you think? Good stuff, right?" He secretly prayed that his cousin would respond to the pastor's invitation to receive Jesus Christ as his personal Savior. He decided to leave the issue with God.

Brandon itched his right ear for several seconds then replied, "Interesting."

Freddy recognized his physiognomy. His cousin was processing the sermon.

But he didn't respond to the altar call.

* * *

The pizza parlor was mobbed. Kathy was elected the 'spotter' to find a table while Freddy and Brandon went to the counter to place the order. One large pepperoni pizza and three colas. In the providence of God, within seven minutes a table became available. Kathy shot a praise to God for his expediency and added that she wanted to be mightily used of the Lord. *She would not be disappointed.*

Brandon sat across from Kathy and ogled at her for several minutes until she interrupted his gaze by saying, "Brandon, what did your think about the pastor's sermon?"

Brandon silently shifted back and forth in his seat for a moment to gather his thoughts. "Can't you people talk of anything else but rebellion and sin? I couldn't sit through that week after week," he complained. "I have never been to church and now you're trying to pressure me into this Jesus revolution!"

"Your right," Kathy said, "but maybe there's more to this than you think. I believe the Lord brought you here today so that you would settle your sin problem with Jesus and become a Christian."

"Sin problem?" Brandon asked. "Become a Christian? What do you do for fun? You don't drink, you don't smoke or do weed, R-rated movies are out and you don't party. Well now after that, I can't think of a thing to say about your—" he paused then whispered vehemently, "—belief system so no, I don't want to become a Christian!"

Kathy reached over and clutched his hand. "Brandon, we are all sinners in God's sight, but he sent Jesus to take on your sin at Calvary so that you would be forgiven and live a life that honors God."

Brandon was speechless. He could not believe what he was hearing.

"Brandon, are you judging us because we choose to live a life that honors God?" Kathy asked. "Freddy, you and I are going to pray for Brandon right now," she said definitely.

Brandon couldn't believe what he was hearing and he wanted to run.

Fortunately the pizza arrived. *They ate in silence.*

* * *

Paul and Donna decided to wait a few days before they called Tommy and Patty to see how Brandon was doing. They were searching the Word of God together each evening asking for divine guidance.

Monday morning arrived and the alarm by Brandon's bed went off at 6:30 A.M. He didn't want breakfast at this ungodly hour nor did he think he should have to do physical labor for his keep. Unexpectedly, uncle Tommy stuck his head in the doorway and said, "Time to get up young man! We have a full day ahead!"

When Brandon walked out of his bedroom he noticed Freddy and his brothers getting ready for school and muttered under his breath things that should not be repeated.

* * *

Brandon didn't realize how big his uncle's construction business was. They were involved in a new development of houses and everyone had a task to be completed. Brandon was given a pair of work gloves and told to empty all the wood used for setting concrete foundations from a truck. He had a problem with it. "Are you kidding me?" he asked the foreman. "By myself?"

"Yes," the foreman replied, "and place it on lot number twelve."

By the end of the day Brandon was sweaty, hungry, and angry. Who would choose to do all this heavy labor? Certainly not him. *I'll talk to uncle Tommy tonight*, he reasoned.

After dinner Brandon asked to speak to his uncle. "Well, how was your first day?" his uncle asked.

"Well, that's what I wanted to talk to you about," Brandon replied. "This heavy labor is not for me. We're rich so we can pay you for having me stay here."

"Young man," Uncle Tommy replied with a smile. "Sit down while we talk. I want to give it to you straight." Brandon nodded and took the closest chair.

"First of all," his uncle began. "You are not rich but your parents are rich. You personally have no assets and let me remind you that it was your parent's idea for you to come and stay with us."

Brandon squirmed in his chair. "Okay, so that true, but I'm sure my parents didn't have in mind my sawing and carrying 2 X 4s, floating concrete and putting up drywall."

"Oh, my, you've learned something of the construction business!" his uncle replied mockingly. "I suggest you call your parents and see if they think you are being abused." Tommy then stood up and walked into another room.

"Well, what did your parents say?" uncle Tommy asked after an hour.

"I don't want to discuss it," Brandon snapped.

"That's fine with me," his uncle replied. "Just be ready for work tomorrow morning at our regular time."

The next morning Brandon was in a foul mood at work. He smelled weed on one of the other workers and asked if he could buy some. One of the workers immediately helped him out by driving him to his stash house. No sooner did they arrive at the house when the police surrounded the house and they were both arrested.

"Where's Brandon?" Tommy asked his foreman when he arrived at the site.

"Unknown," his foreman replied. "I'm told he went off with one of the other workers and didn't come back."

Could he have conjured some way to get back to my house? he wondered. He called Patty. "He's not here. He's been arrested for buying drugs," she replied wearily.

"I'll be right home."

Upon arrival Patty rushed to meet him in the driveway. "What are we going to do?" she fretted.

"I called my brother on the way home and went over a plan to shake Brandon up a bit," Tommy explained. "He's in complete agreement. We're going to let him stay in lockup for a while. Then I will go and tell him the outcome of his foolish act that may land him in Janesville Detention, better known as 'juvey.' Let's pray we scare the hell out of him. Now I need to call our pastor and get everyone praying for Brandon."

When Kathy heard that Brandon had been arrested, she felt the Holy Spirit telling her to go to the jail and talk to him. Since Brandon was in holding, they let Kathy in to speak with him. "What are you doing here?" Brandon asked, embarrassed that she saw him there.

"I came to find out if you understood any more clearly your sin problem," she replied in a subdued tone. "The Holy Spirit guided me to come and talk to you—" she paused and then said gruffly after registering the look on his face, "—Brandon, why are you so upset with your life?"

"Because no one cares about me," he said wearily. "My parents are so focused on their careers and all the money it brings that they think they can buy me off with an eBike and computer and other stuff. My uncle Tommy and Aunt Patty are only doing my parents a favor by getting me out of their hair."

"I guess you don't know your aunt and uncle as well as I do through your cousin Freddy," Kathy replied. "They are the most caring family and they would not have agreed to help if they didn't really want to.

"But neither your parents nor relatives can fill the void that is within you. Only Jesus can and he went to the cross to prove his love for you. He promises to never leave you or forsake you," she explained as she crossed her arms. "That's pretty cool, right?

"I want you to promise me that you will at least be open to what God has for your life. We all have a purpose on an individual basis, but we also have a combined purpose and that is to honor God with our lives. The Bible says, ' . . . you will seek me in your affliction,' so I will pray for you to seek Jesus and get right with him." She held his hand for a moment then left.

Uncle Tommy thought hard on his nephew Brandon on his way to visit him. His inner spirit provoked him to call his attorney and he was glad he did. When he arrived at the juvie lock up, ready to give him the riot act for his behavior, he saw that he was alone and sad. He changed his mind. "I'm here to take you home," he said. "I had my attorney call the judge and they are letting you off with a warning and probation."

Brandon walked into his home with slumping shoulders full of sadness. But his mom and dad ran up to him, throwing their arms around him and confessing over and over how much they loved him. Brandon looked over at his uncle in bewilderment, but uncle Tommy just smiled as if all would be alright.

An hour later Paul and Donna sat down with Brandon. "We have had our priorities all wrong and this family has suffered because of it," his dad lamented. "Your mom and I have been going to church these last few weeks and reading the Bible together. We have come to a few decisions: One, is your mother is going to quit her job to become the wife and mother she always wanted to be. Two, as a family we have a way to go but we are willing to search for God's answers. Are you willing to join us?"

When they looked at Brandon, they both saw the real Brandon, the son who looked with expectancy to the parents he loved.

LOST AND FOUND

RENEWED HOPE CHRISTIAN COUNSELING CENTER

*N*ow that I'm here, I'm glad that I listened to my pastor who urged me to talk things out with someone who can help me, Lauren thought. *I believe that if I speak to a Christian counselor who offers biblical advice it will enable me to adjust to life and handle my problems better.*

The Renewed Hope Christian counseling center was part of the First Christian Church of Sunrise, Florida, employing three licensed counselors with advanced degrees. The ministry offered biblical counseling to both members and non-members who sought God's guidance for the problems of life that the world or they themselves could not seem to solve.

Lauren walked into the office, signed in then took her seat. Seconds later she checked her cell phone for new emails then noticed the magnificent nature photos on the surrounding walls. Staring at the intricate detail of the macro view of the Passiflora flower and the telescopic photos of the Pillars of Creation in the constellation Serpens brought a sense of comfort. *God's handiwork gives me peace*, she thought.

"Mrs. Sanderson," the receptionist said, "can I see you for a moment?"

Lauren walked to the counter. "For your first visit, you will be seeing Doctor Madison who will be with you in just a few moments. In the meantime let's review your insurance and medical background." Lauren complied then returned to her seat. Ten minutes later she was escorted to Dr. Madison's office.

His office didn't look anything like a corporate office. It looked more like a living room with two recliners, a sofa, a corner table with a small coffee urn, cups and cupcakes. Off to one side was a chair in front of a modest desk with a Bible on top: all accentuating the closeness of the room. On the wall next to his bookcases was a canvas portrait of Christ holding a wounded lamb with a bible verse under the painting. *Wow, looks cozy*, she thought as she sat in one of the recliners.

Moments later Dr. Madison walked in, grabbed a folding chair from behind his desk and then sat down in front of Lauren. "Hello, I'm Dr. Madison, but you can call me Billy," he said as he extended his hand.

"I've heard only good things about this center at church, Billy," Lauren said after shaking his hand. "And yes, good things about you as well," she added with a smile. For her to smile was a God-thing. After years of mental abuse by her husband along with raising two disenfranchised children, and the added stress of financial mismanagement, it wasn't until God stepped in was she able to smile.

He glanced down at her input file then said, " I note that you have been recently widowed. How can I help you?"

Lauren took note that this man before her reminded her of both a professional medical doctor and a conservative pastor all rolled into one. He looked in his 40s and was clean shaving with just the beginning of a receding hairline. He had on a suit and tie, with the modern-day tan shoes. *He takes his calling very seriously as a voice of the Holy Spirit*, she thought.

"I have been reviewing my life these past few days. Is it healthy to review your life for reasons why you made the decision you made and why you didn't reverse those decisions when they made you angry and full of despair? Did I really deserve my lot in life—?" She paused to reflect, while Dr. Madison assumed the opening salvo was simply rhetorical.

He nodded while greatly stirred and said, "I'm with you. Go on and give me more background!"

Lauren complied. "Looking back I was a happy child, comfortable in my own skin. I was an average student in school but I tended to be on the shy side especially if compared to my three younger siblings.

"Friends were always important to me and as a result when I graduated high school, my friends and I wanted to go on an adventure. We set out on a road trip from New York to San Diago where we all got jobs where we had many exciting experiences. We stayed one year and then we got a little homesick and decided it was time to go back home where I found a new job. It was a wonderful experience and one that I will always treasure." She paused and shrugged her shoulders while musing for a few seconds then continued. "I have always been the romantic dreamer and when I met my husband I thought all my dreams had come true. They say 'love is blind' but love can also cause us to be deaf as well. We ignore any negative signs and continue on with the fairytale and my wedding was just that. I couldn't have been happier—" Noticing that Dr. Madison was taking selective notes she paused. Then: "Why didn't it last?" she continued. "Was it a lack of communication where my husband didn't really want children and I desperately did? Was the responsibility of raising a family too much for him? When he lost his job, was that the game-changer that I didn't support like I should have?

"I only know that I became the reason his life wasn't perfect. He started drinking more and this should have been a red flag as his mother was an alcoholic and became a total recluse. By this time we had two children who he rarely bothered with except to criticize.

"Of course every time the children didn't excel it was my fault because he had married someone so stupid. A few years of this and you start to believe it's true and you don't realize you're an abused woman. Not physically, but mentally. The silver lining in those days was I had a family that loved me, parents and siblings that all lived close by. I found myself full of doubt and confusion and considered myself unworthy—I was lost, but then I was found!"

Dr. Madison raised his hand to ask a question. He sounded amazed. "What does that last phrase mean? Help me put that in context."

Lauren nodded. "Well, one of my sisters told me she found the Lord and he was her Savior. He forgave all her sins and she experienced a freedom to love and serve him as never before. I have to admit that I was very curious.

"Shortly afterwards my sister and her husband started a bible study in their home and that's where my journey in life with the Lord began. One of the first things I heard was that Jesus took my place on the cross to give me a place in heaven and that my happiness depended on happenings, but my joy depended on Jesus—" She paused momentarily to refresh her memory then: "I began to have an inner quest for truth so I began to study the Bible that was new to me and after one week I realized my need for a personal Savior and so I prayed to receive the forgiveness he offered. That's when I realized that I was once lost but now found by Jesus."

Dr. Madison stood up and smiled at Lauren. "I'm really impressed," he said then tapped his wristwatch. "Having a relationship with Jesus and placing our trust in his word makes all the difference in the world when it comes to family problems. I will give you an assignment to complete at home and we will pick this up where you left off on our talk next session. We're good?"

"We're good," she replied with a sigh of relief after recounting part of her life's journey.

He took a peek at her file then added, "When we meet next time we will talk about your relationship with your late husband and your kids," he affirmed. "Now for your assignment, I want you to read, study, and meditate on these two bible verses and give me your explanation and application." He handed her a sheet from his notepad. I would like you to put it in writing so you can use it as sort of a journal of our getting together meetings."

Lauren glanced down at the note that read: Psalm 34:1; Psalm 103:7. "No problem," she said. Then as she began to walk to the door added, "Meeting you—even though I did most of the talking—was a relief to me. I really needed someone with your qualifications to hear my story."

"It was a blessing meeting and listening to you," he replied while shaking her hand.

* * *

When Lauren opened the front door of her three-bedroom condo she heard the TV on with the volume blasting the rerun of the last NFL football game. Once inside the living room she recognized the recurring scene. Her 32-year-old son, Douglas, was sitting on the sofa opposite the TV with his feet on the coffee table eating from a bag of potato chips. "What's the latest with the job search?" she asked fighting off her immediate impulse to argue with him over his lethargic attitude that she believed he inherited from his father.

"Same," he replied, pressing a button on the TV remote to lower the volume.

Lauren bit her lower lip as she walked over to him and took the TV remote from his hand then pressed the OFF button. Then she sat down at the far end of the sofa. "I would like more details if you don't mind," she replied as the tension in the room heightened. Then she shot a look over at the kitchen sink and saw the dirty dishes stacked up. "I thought I asked you this morning to load the dirty dishes in the dishwasher." She shook her head and added, " And did you vacuum out your room like I asked?"

"Don't fuss," he replied casually. "I'll get to it before the end of the day."

Her nerves were getting raw. She cradled her face in her hands in an effort to attenuate the rising anxiety. *This is the legacy I've inherited from his father.* "We have one hour before dinner. Get up and vacuum your room right now or there will be no dinner for you!" she exclaimed.

"Fine—if it's an emergency," he replied defiantly. He then gave off a long snuffing sound as he wiped his nose on his shirt. After that he rose from the sofa and shuffled his feet to the hall closet to get the vacuum being extremely spiteful to slowly close his bedroom door behind him. It was fifteen minutes later before Lauren heard the vacuum running.

When it came time for dinner to be served he filled his plate and carried it into his bedroom to eat alone.

* * *

In the middle of the night Lauren awoke when her conscience truly troubled her. *Have I given Douglas the love a mother should have for her son? Have I been the godly example a Christian mother should have toward him? Have I sat down with him and shared the gospel and plan of salvation?* No, the answer came back. *But as long as there's life, there's hope. It's not enough to know the facts of salvation, you must also know the Savior,* she reminded herself.

She reached over and turned on the bedroom light then quickly went to the bathroom then returned to her bed and caught a glimpse of a pictured framed of her daughter embracing her granddaughter. A plethora of memories flooded her mind. *I know now, she thought, why Melinda married so young and moved out of state—to get away from her father and me to an extent because I now realize both my children blame me for putting up with their abusive father as long as I did.* Fifteen minutes later she shot a prayer up to the Lord and rehearsed several bible verses in her mind. But it wasn't until after she actually read three psalms in her bedside bible did she finally fall asleep.

At eight o'clock in the morning Lauren woke up to the sound of unrelenting rain splashing against her bedroom windows. "Ugh!" she muttered. *Wouldn't you know it would be on the day I'm scheduled for work.* As a volunteer at the Broward County Hospital Lauren's role was an intake receptionist in the outpatient services department three days a week. It was more of a ministry than anything else since the Lord gave her ample opportunities to encourage those facing surgery for that day.

But before she would go to work she had to take care of some business at home.

Knock! Knock! Knock! Doug heard in his bedroom as he lay semi-awake in his bed. "Time to rise and shine before mom goes to work," he heard. He expelled a groan when he looked at the clock on his wall.

"What's up, mom?" he cried out as he fumbled out of his bed.

"I want to talk to you before I leave," Lauren replied with a soothing tone.

Seconds later his door opened. He stood in the doorway scratching his head.

"Sit down with me and have a cup of coffee," his mother said as tears welled up in her eyes. She determined in her heart to convey a spirit of love and peace to her son. "I have been thinking about our relationship and it is in my heart to help you in your life, but it's not a one-way street. You have to be willing to help yourself as well," she began.

Douglas nodded curtly and smiled blandly and said after sipping his coffee, "What do you suggest?"

"Well, I don't think it's a good idea for you to stay home and simply apply for work on the computer for a few hours, then take the rest of the day watching the TV. You need to dress professionally and take your updated resume and go knock on some doors.

"You have a college education," she explained, "and are young enough where you can begin a career and get the most out of life. Working does have its rewards—" For a moment she hesitated about bringing up the subject but decided to trust the Lord and said, "And then there's the issue of you going to church. You know that I'm very content in the church I'm attending and believe God is using our pastor to convey the truth and many people are coming to a personal relationship with Christ through his ministry. For me, I believe it has really deepened my walk with Jesus because I attend a bible study and have made many Christian friends at this church and that combination in turn enables me to deal with the everyday problems of life." Reaching over and clutching his hand she added, "Jesus is the answer to my problems as well as yours. By being part of the family of God you can share your life with others your age, meet other

Christian men and women and experience fulfillment in your life. So will you please think on these things today while I'm gone?"

He itched his right ear while thinking how to respond. "Yes, I'll think about it," he said.

Then his mom left for work.

When she returned home his bedroom door was closed. She got the message: *I'm not interested.*

* * *

RENEWED HOPE CHRISTIAN COUNSELING CENTER

This has been a long tough week between sessions, Lauren thought. *Dealing with my loneliness and my son's antics is taking a toll on me*, she believed as she pulled into the counselor's parking lot.

I'm not quite as nervous as I was before my first session, Lauren reminded herself as she, once again, stared at the nature photographs on Dr. Madison's office wall. One in particular caught her attention. It was of a male and female African lion snuggling together, both watching their next prey off in the distance. *How did he get this? What timing!* she wondered. She saw an award ribbon attached to the photo. It appeared that the photographer won the grand prize in a contest conducted by a national photo lab.

Thinking back to her first session she thought: *he seems to be a nice guy, listening to my tale of woe and the Holy Spirit confirms to me that he can help.*

Breaking into her thoughts the receptionist said, "Mrs. Sanderson, Dr. Madison will see you now."

Lauren walked up to the counter and asked the receptionist as she pointed to them, "Who took all those nature photos?"

"Doctor Madison," she replied with a smile. "It's his form of therapy. On his days off he travels into the wilderness, or to butterfly habitats, or the zoo, or plays with his telescope and takes the photos. Good stuff, right?"

"Outstanding!" Lauren replied. "They give one a greater appreciation for God's creative hand." Then she walked into Dr. Madison's office.

"Your nature photographs are a pleasant representation of God's glory," she said as she pointed toward the waiting room.

"I appreciate that," he replied. "God's creative design inspires me. The photography gives me time away from my ministry and gives me perspective." he added as he escorted her to a chair then went and sat behind his desk.

"So how was your week?"

"Both good and bad," she replied while smiling mirthlessly.

"By the look on your face it seems it was mostly bad," he replied while glancing at his notes. "Tell me how you did on the assignment then we'll get into the week's events."

Lauren pulled out her cell phone and tapped the *notes* app. "In Psalm 34:1, David expresses his praise for the Lord and blesses him despite the difficulties he was experiencing when fleeing from his enemies. For me the application is that I should praise the Lord despite my difficulties and not have a complaining spirit.

"In Psalm 103:7, David explains the difference between asking God to demonstrate his ways instead of his acts. For me I'm reminded to ask the Lord how I can get to know him more intimately during my trying events instead of asking him to do more for me like taking away the things that bother me and asking him to make my life better."

Dr. Madison nodded in approval. "That's a good rendering of the text, and hopefully it will help you apply those gems into your daily life. The key to those verses is that we keep our eyes on Jesus, not on the problem. He is the great 'fixer' of our problems." Then he made a few notations in her file. "Okay, now tell me about the 'good and the bad.'"

"This past week was part of the outworking of my life's history," she began. "After my salvation experience that I related to you last week, my life at home did not change. I was changed but my surrounding conditions did not change. I appealed to my husband telling him Jesus could give us a second chance and initially he was interested but I saw little difference and little fruit.

"However, I put my children in Christian school and tried to set the proper example for them. Shortly afterwards one of my sisters encouraged me to take the needed exam to get a job at the school but it troubled me. I had already doubted I could pass it but she insisted that was not true and even if I did fail the first time I could take it again. But I didn't fail the first time and the job became a lifeline for me.

"The way I took to the job made me realize that I had believed the lie that I couldn't succeed. I thrived as a person and made lifelong friends.

We all have a story but as friends we were there for each other, encouraging each other and having so much fun together. I was grateful that the Lord had found me because I was so lost. My worldview changed, my personality changed, my goals changed, and my love for Jesus continued to increase. But my relationship with my husband did not improve." *She fell silent momentarily.*

"But the good was that when he became sick and his condition worsened, he needed me more—I guess as a nursemaid—but I took it from God as an opportunity to love him more, thinking that if anything happened to him, I would not want a guilty conscience for treating him the way he treated me. So I asked the Lord to give me the needed grace to minister to him. During the time of his debilitating condition he began to use our son as an errand boy who would fetch his so-called needs and in turn our son soon resigned to the fact that he could not seek employment because he was needed by his father.

"Then when my husband died, my son was unable to undo the damage my husband put upon him so he simply gave up on life and now—the bad is—" she paused and took a deep breath as her melancholy attitude began to dominate her session. "Since he's living with me at this time and has adopted many of my husband's traits, we are having a difficult time at home."

"And your daughter?" he asked pointedly as he digested her report.

"Melinda is Melinda," she replied as she steepled her fingers. "I know she has her own family now so I don't expect any support from her regarding her brother because they don't get along. I think the real problem with her is that she—and to a degree her brother—blame me for staying with their father and putting up with his abuse."

"You've traveled a tough journey but I will say that in my estimation you have handled it well because you are depending on the Lord more now than ever before and I urge you to continue to do so.

"As far as your son and daughter is concerned," he advised, "your daughter because of the distance is no longer in your field of influence. So I suggest that you not interfere in her life, simply let the Lord deal with her—" he paused to collect his thoughts as he looked at her eyes dancing with anticipation so he leaned closer and said, "Your son, considering he lives with you is an anomaly that once again, only the good Lord can fix. However I must ask, do you think he would be open to counsel?"

"Um, I don't think so. At least not now. I don't think he's ready," she replied sadly. "In the future—who knows?"

"Of a certainty, we don't want to interfere with God's timing," Dr. Madison counseled. "But for your comfort, I quote a wise sage who said, 'The problem in getting great things from God is holding on for the last half hour.' So kindly ask the Lord for an extra amount of grace to hold you until God acts."

* * *

When Lauren got home and opened the door to her condo she was surprised to see her son vacuuming the living room . . .

CHRISTIAN
MINISTRY

THE ESCORT

T he Parkview Christian Church in downtown Jacksonville was well
known in Florida for its uncompromising stand on conservative
doctrine, its evangelical outreach, its discipleship programs, and its size. It
was in the church vernacular, a megachurch. It quickly earned the title of
a 'flagship' church in the denomination that was all attributed to its pastor
of twenty years. Pastor Marcus Fielding, at the young age of forty-eight,
with a doctorate in Biblical Studies from Dallas Theological Seminary was
determined to hold fast to the biblical principles of the first century church
amidst the ever-changing winds of study in today's churches. His congregation welcomed his stand and stood behind him.

Pastor Marcus was well known for his treatment of both the multi-
cultural population in Jacksonville as well as his treatment of the varied
age groups that attended his church. He treated the teenager as well as
the seniors according to their spiritual needs and even extended multi-
language services for the aliens that were becoming more frequent as the
nation's borders became increasingly porous. To him Jesus' arms were
extended to all who seek him.

God had gifted him with an extraordinary memory. Despite the size of
his congregation he remembered, for the most part, their first names while
often struggling or pinching his wife to remind him of their last names and
those of their children. Altogether, both him and his wife, Jenny, they were
a formidable couple to head up such a blessed church.

*But funerals were a problem for him when he really didn't know about
the decedent's relationship with Jesus.*

"Marcus, you need to decide how you're going to handle this memorial service," Jenny asked him curiously as she sat in front of his desk. "Since Marion has been a part of our church for a little more than a year, involved in our woman's ministry, our sports program, part of a senior's Sunday School group, and in reaching out to the unwed mothers—it's a no-brainer when it comes to how your eulogy of her will go."

"But the crucial issues have never been approached from my perspective, my love," he replied smoothly. He counted very heavily on her spiritual, tactical, and emotional input when it came to church complications. "The truth of the matter is—" he paused to collect his thoughts, "—since she died so suddenly I'm not really sure she was a believer who trusted Christ as her Savior. I recognize her involvement in church activities, but I never really had the opportunity to sit with her because she was so involved in different aspects of our church, and now that the family asked me to perform the funeral service—I need to know for sure or else I'm going in another direction. It will be a generic or standard funeral service."

Jenny closed her eyes momentarily and put a palm to her forehead. "I know her husband, Reggie, wasn't really involved in our church, but can you treat this as a non-believing funeral without knowing for sure?"

Marcus expelled a sigh. "I have until tomorrow to conduct the service so I'm simply going to petition the Lord and his Spirit overnight for direction."

* * *

PINE MANOR FUNERAL HOME

Pastor Marcus was still ambivalent during his morning prayer time about how to minister at Marion's memorial service. Jenny bowed out of the decision-making process relying on God to direct her husband, hoping that his decision would not in any way polarize their church's congregation. She knew it would be a tough call for him.

But the Lord had a plan that neither one knew.

Pastor Marcus and Jenny noticed that the parking lot of the Pine Manor Funeral Home was filling up quickly when they arrived. "You're going to have a difficult time getting Reggie aside before you begin the service," Jenny said in the form of a prayer request.

"I have to!" he replied with clear precision.

Just inside the entrance to the funeral home, Reggie stood alongside the podium containing the guest sign-in list and smiled with handshakes as the people walked in. Pastor Marcus nodded to Jenny then walked to Reggie. "Can I steal you away for a few minutes?" he asked politely. Reggie nodded and motioned to the funeral home arranger in his monochromatic attire who took his place at the welcome podium.

Pastor Marcus was aware that Marion's husband was a non-attender when it came to worship or bible studies. Reggie had met pastor Marcus several times at church gatherings and festivals at his wife's behest, but never spent any personal or private time with him.

This would be the first.

Once inside the funeral arranger's office, pastor Marcus gestured to Reggie to take a seat. Once they were both seated pastor Marcus started to tear-up then took out a handkerchief from his rear pocket and dried his eyes. "Reggie," he said, turning on his soothing voice, his pastor's consoling voice, "you asked me to speak at Marion's service, and it's a joy to do so because I want to bring comfort to those who are grieving over her death, especially you since you've been married for over thirty years," he began. "So help me here to say the right things in front of all those who came out to show their respects to both Marion and you."

"No problem," Reggie replied and wiggled slightly in his seat as if he were expecting a question he wouldn't be able to answer.

"That's good," Pastor Marcus replied then: "In all the time that Marion has been at our church, has she ever shared with you some of the things we teach or preached about on Sunday or Wednesday night bible study?" He took a huge leap. He knew it, but it had to be asked.

Stiffening slightly. "Like what for instance?"

"Well," Pastor Marcus probed casually, "like things about the bible's view on life or heaven, or sin, or prophecy, or what happens when a person receives Christ as their Savior? Or are there any changes in a person's life once they receive Christ?"

Reggie sighed blissfully. "Well to tell you the truth, in all the time she's been at your church—she's was keeping busy as a bee and appeared to be very happy. We were getting along a lot better."

"Have you talked about what happens when someone dies?"

Reggie meditated momentarily on that question. "Well, she men-tioned that she hoped the person would go directly to heaven, but she also thought that the person might have to spend some time in purgatory before getting there."

That told Pastor Marcus what he needed to know.

Pastor Marcus slapped Reggie on the knee and said, "I see. Well, we better get back in there since the service starts in fifteen minutes."

Reggie nodded in relief and followed him out to the parlor.

*　*　*

Pastor Marcus waited until the late arrivals paid their respects to Marion's body in the casket then nodded to the funeral home arranger who then approached the podium to introduce him to the audience. After being introduced, pastor Marcus did a quick visual survey of the partakers and realized there were many from her senior's group along with non-members of his church who came to comfort and console Reggie. It was then, together with his conversation with Reggie, that the spirit of God confirmed to him the content of his eulogy. "We welcome Marion's church members, family, and friends to her memorial service," he began with an uplifting tone. "It is with heartfelt sorrow that we pray for God to nurture Reggie and his family who—along with our church—will miss Marion dearly.

"Marion was a wonderful asset to our church who participated in many ministries and brought comfort to other members in her senior's group as well as to her Sunday School teacher. Marion, along with her works will be deeply missed—" He hesitated, assessed, and then added, "The Bible says, 'For God so loved the world that he gave his only begotten Son that whoever believes in him should not perish but have everlasting life . . . and by their fruit you shall know them.'"

He paused.

Silence.

He pointed into the audience and with a parallel wave added poignantly, "If you have not received Jesus as your personal Savior, I implore you to do so today! He is the only way to heaven." He pointed to the back of the room and added, "I'll be available after this service if anyone would like to know more about being born-again and having their sins forgiven and beginning a life-long relationship with Christ."

The feeling of power in the room was almost palpable. Pastor Marcus could tell there were those who were perplexed and others with mixed emotions over his presentation, feeling that there were certain things that he omitted. When pastor Marcus looked at Reggie he could see that he wasn't really interested. He just had that silly smile-and-everything-will-be-fine on his face. But God's spirit confirmed to Marcus that what he said would cause many to come to the only conclusion possible. They needed Jesus in their lives in order to get to heaven.

After the funeral assistant gave the dismissal of the service a small group surrounded pastor Marcus before going to the gravesite. They had many questions.

* * *

On the car ride to church for Sunday worship Pastor Marcus' fourteen-year-old son, Jason, with a real casual, laid-back gesture said, "I've been keeping score and yesterday's funeral with Marion Clark was the fourth funeral this year, and it's only July. How come so many people are dying in our church?"

Jenny shot a look at her husband when the question was asked who then shrugged his shoulders as he drove and replied, "I certainly have no control over who lives and dies—that's the Lord's business." Then he added, "I'm not in the position to explain or defend, but your mother and I realize that we do have a lot of seniors in our church—over two hundred—and we have come to expect that each year some will die.

"But as it happens, in view of the number of deaths we've had here at Parkview this year, and they have not all been our seniors, I've decided to speak on that subject today in my sermon to encourage our congregation. So—" he paused and glanced at his wife, "—afterwards Jason, come and ask me what you thought of it. Okay?"

Jason blinked, "Will do."

* * *

Parkview's contemporary service was a big draw for the youth and millennials with the drums, guitars and modern-day songs led by a song trio. The seniors preferred the traditional service since the hymns were from the old hymn book they were familiar with and there were less guitars and no drums, just piano and organ music along with the choir. Thus, Parkview offered two Sunday services in an effort to meet both groups' needs. The downside, according to Jenny was that there was little mingling of the two and split service encouraged separation which is what pastor Marcus was determined to avoid. His system was that he would deliver the same sermon to both groups while encouraging joint fellowship and prayer meetings.

"What's the title of today's sermon?" Jenny asked casually as they pulled into the church parking lot.

He smiled at her and replied, "The Horizontal Dash."

She knew within herself that he had given that sermon before with a dramatic outcome, but not without a squeeze to the congregation. "Ooook'y, I'll be praying for God's best."

"Remember it is better to light a candle than to curse the darkness," he replied with a nod.

* * *

Many of the seniors that attended Marion Clark's funeral approached pastor Marcus the moment he walked into the sanctuary to conduct the traditional service. Some had questions, others simply wanted to express their appreciation for his ministry at the funeral.

Within minutes he excused himself to address the choir leader to make a slight change in the hymn lineup to include his favorite, *Redeemed*. In his mind this would be an appropriate invitation hymn after his sermon. Then he went to the head deacon who made the announcements at the end of the sermon and reversed the order. He wanted the Word of God to be the last things on the congregation's mind, not the church's schedule for the upcoming week.

"The title of my sermon for today is going to be '*The Horizontal Dash*.' I know your church bulletin and schedule has a different title, but I believe God's Spirit is moving and inspired me to change it.

"So please turn in your Bible's to James chapter four and let us read verses thirteen to fifteen . . . " he paused to allow them to locate the text in their bibles. Then he read it from his aloud:

> "Come now, you who say, 'Today or tomorrow we will go to such and such a city, spend a year there, buy and sell, and make a profit; whereas you do not know what will happen tomorrow. For what is our life? It is even a vapor and appears for a little time and then vanishes away. Instead you ought to say, 'if the Lord wills, we shall live and do this and that.'"

Then he closed his bible and set it on the pulpit and said with piercing eyes, "Before Jenny and I were married and I was in seminary, I worked part time for an insurance company in their claims division. One claim remains in my memory to today because it had a profound influence on my spiritual life. It revolved around a man who owned a gravestone memorial company who filed a claim for a small fire in his basement and I was asked to investigate.

"After reviewing the damage for my report he took me on a tour of his company and I found it very interesting. In one corner of his shop was what I called a 'chamber' that was surrounded by layers of foam rubber and in the middle of the chamber was the granite tombstone that had yet to be inscribed with the information of the decedent. Covering the tombstone was a rubber stencil with the deceased's information that included the name, a short bible verse or one of their famous lines—" he paused and said abruptly: "—and then there was the date of birth separated by a horizontal line to the date of death. The two-inch horizontal line represented the entire time the person spent here on earth.

"Our Bible text in James uses the simile of our life as a vapor. The meaning is that we are here for a short time then suddenly we are gone. Because our life is so brief—" he paused to emphasize his next point— "what we do for the Lord is all that matters! Anything else is as Paul says is , 'stones, wood, hay, and straw.' So make your life count for Christ so that your heavenly crowns and rewards may be great. When people look at your life they should be reading the bible by your thoughts, words, and deeds. My question to you is: what version are they reading?

"After showing me the tombstone to be inscribed, the shopkeeper advised me to back away from the chamber. Then he showed me what resembled a shotgun filled with pellets that would be fired at the tombstone that would in fact perform the engraving. He handed me a set of earplugs and after I inserted them he then fired the gun at the tombstone. BOOM!

"It was amazing! He removed the rubber covering and behold, etched in the granite was all that really mattered about this man's life. His name, a brief inscription, and dates of life and death.

"The firing of the shotgun to etch the tombstone reminded me of life's difficulties, they are the 'shots' that are fired on us in life that turn out to be an important part of our testimony. Prayerfully your life will reflect what you believe."

He paused momentarily.

"What we do for the Lord in our lifetime is all that matters! When we consider eternity and that little horizontal line we realize how little time we have on the earth." He motioned to his music minister that they needed to play the invitation hymn, *Redeemed*, and ended with a closing prayer. Jenny smiled at him and counted that more than ten people from the church came forward for prayer. His son, Jason, gave him a thumb up.

* * *

It was three weeks later that the need for visitation came in. Visitation was an important part of pastor Marcus' ministry that he divided up with his deacons. Visiting young, growing families brought joy and fulfillment, while visiting those who were terminally ill brought a different element to his ministry, that of bringing comfort to the sick and to friends and family who would face the inevitable of losing the loved one. Unless the terminally ill person was a Christian. Then things were different.

Visiting George Lambert, his long-time deacon suffering with fourth-stage lung cancer brought him an abundance of joy. The man had such a positive outlook despite his terminal condition that pastor Marcus was not only uplifted in the spirit after visiting him but inspired to continue to preach on the subject of the living looking forward to eternal life with Christ.

Today things would be different.

"George has been asking for you, pastor," George's wife Betsy said the minute he walked in the door. "He's not doing so well today."

Pastor Marcus recognized the sign. When a sick member asked for the pastor it meant the Lord was calling that person home to heaven to be with him. Today would be George's day. "Bring me to him," Pastor Marcus replied as he began to fill up with emotions.

Surprisingly, George's bedroom was bright from refulgent sunlight and cheery with other deacons and family members mulling around the room encouraging Betsy with both words and promises to be available to help her when the time would come. She was being uplifted despite her fears.

The minute pastor Marcus walked in George saw him then held up his hand from the bed and said wearily, "I've been waiting for you pastor." Pastor Marcus extended his hand and grasped George's who then said, "I remember your sermon on the Escort—" then he swallowed hard and added, "—well mine is here and he's calling me but was waiting for you so I could say goodbye."

Pastor Marcus bent over and kissed his forehead. Then he glanced over at Betsy standing against a wall who began to sob the minute she heard her husband say goodbye. "I'm here for you George," he said with eyes blurred with tears, "and so are all those here in your bedroom. We're praying you through to heaven. We're here until Jesus takes you."

George smiled then nodded. Seconds later he pointed his other hand to the wall and said joyfully, "Betsy, stand aside, my Escort is here. He's standing at the foot of heaven's ladder, beckoning me to come to him." He gulped then exclaimed, "Jesus, I love you!" He took a deep breath and sounding amazed uttered, "I have to go—" Everyone stared at Betsy and raised their hands to heaven then to George who had the joy of the Lord look on his face while his body was suddenly stilled.

Then he was gone.

* * *

PARKVIEW CHRISTIAN CHURCH

Pastor Marcus stood in front of George's American flagged-draped casket and was delighted that there was such a good turnout from the church body to honor their deacon and beloved brother in the Lord. Betty along with other members of George's family sat in the first pew while pastor Marcus' family sat on the other side. The rest of the church was full.

Pastor Marcus signaled the organ player then prayed before opening his Bible. "Our text today is Acts chapter seven where we will read verses fifty-four through sixty. Please stand as we read from God's Word:

> "'When they heard these things, they were cut to the heart, and they gnashed on him with their teeth. But he, being full of the Holy Ghost, looked steadfastly into heaven, and saw the glory of God, and Jesus standing on the right hand of God. And said, 'Behold, I see the heavens opened, and the Son of Man standing on the right hand of God.' Then they cried out with a loud voice, and stopped their ears, and ran upon him with one accord, and cast him out of the city, and stoned him. And the witnesses laid down their clothes at a young man's feet, whose name was Saul. And they stoned Stephen, who was calling upon God, and saying, Lord Jesus, receive my spirit. And he kneeled down, and cried with a

loud voice, Lord, lay not this sin to their charge. And when he had said this, he fell asleep."'

He glanced down at his notes then said as he made a sweeping motion with his hand, "Almost everyone fears dying, principally because they face the unknown; they're really not sure of what happens when the body gives up its life. They have some vague notions, suppositions, and clouded religious beliefs about the subject, but when it comes to the finish line, where the rubber meets the road; when they really stop and dwell upon it, either they are really not sure or they are just plain afraid.

"But should it be that way for believer's who know God's promises? A forgiven sinner who knows in advance what lies in wait for him or her? No, it shouldn't be. We who have appropriated Jesus' blood should know that we pass from death unto life with our risen Lord and that this is not a fearful uncertainty, but a documented fact. We will know for sure where we are going.

"To those who are outside of God's forgiveness, their fate is somewhat different, and they should be frightened! The eternal pain and loneliness that awaits them is unimaginable. They will find out that to have received Jesus as their Savior before they died would have been far more sensible than to reject Him. They will see that all of their fears will be realized as they are cast into the bottomless pit, there to remain until the appointed time of the Great White Throne Judgment where they will be convicted of their sin then hurled into the never-ending Lake of Fire. But to those who have trusted Christ, this message is addressed. To those who have wondered or thought about what happens in the moment of transition from death to life, this is addressed. To those who are looking forward to that glorious moment where we meet our Jesus face-to-face, this message is addressed. He promises to be our personal escort to heaven.

"Looking at God's Word in Acts chapter 7, we see a vivid scene of a believer going on to glory. Stephen, a Spirit-filled evangelist, had just delivered a searing Gospel message to the Sanhedrin (the ruling Jewish leaders) where he recounted for them the history of Israel from Joseph in Egypt to David's son, Solomon, building the Temple. He then concentrated his sermon on Jesus being the fulfillment of the Law and the Messianic prophecies and then accused the unbelieving Jews of being stiff-necked murderers with uncircumcised hearts not willing to listen to the truth of God's prophets. When the unbelieving Jews heard this stinging report, they became incensed and reacted accordingly.

"Being convicted of their sin and unbelief without repentance, the mob could only react to this sermon in the flesh and retaliate with striking force, so they killed Stephen to silence him. But did you notice how calm Stephen remained while he was being executed? He was praising God and praying like our friend George did.

"What would you do when an angry mob snarls at you for giving the Gospel, then begins dragging you bodily out of town for a 'lynching'? In the natural man, wouldn't you be inclined to take off as fast as your feet would take you? Or at least get a few good punches in? But here the scene is one of divine composure in the face of a struggle. Why? Because Stephen remembered God's promises to other believers and the patriarchs, that courage would be given to him at a time of trial. Stephen took the promise personally because even at his own execution he was to be strong since God would be with him. So regardless of your trial, whether it be a death situation or a grueling case of perseverance, God promises you courage and peace to enable you to be a witness for Him, and that's what Stephen displayed, God's courage.

"Stephen knew that in the "twinkling of an eye" he would cross over from death unto life. Just as the Rapture of the church occurs in the indivisible instant of time to remove those believers who are alive at the Second Coming, so is it within margin to expect the same treatment and time interval for those believers dying before the Rapture.

"The very moment death came upon Stephen; he was to be in the presence of his Redeemer. He knew that! There was to be no waiting period, purgatory, or 'lay-over,' but an instantaneous change. Is it any wonder that Stephen displayed a holy tranquility at his own murder?"

Pastor Marcus could see that the eyes of his congregation were glued to him. Now he would make a personal application in his closing appeal. "In this wonderful promise, believers are advised not to be troubled since the Father has prepared a heavenly place for us. The promise applies to those who *"fall asleep"* in death before the Second Coming. Falling asleep verses dead, is the term Christ used in Matthew nine when raising the ruler's daughter who had died. Then of course, he used the term when it came to his friend Lazarus in John chapter eleven. *The believers are sleeping not dead.*

"The Old Testament affirms this truth of a personal escort by our Redeemer to His believers who are sleeping where we read in Psalm twenty-three, '... yea, though you walk through the valley of the shadow of death ... fear no evil ... *for I am with you* ...'

"So then, Jesus makes a personal visit to His followers to retrieve them at the moment of death! He escorts us up the ladder to glory and eternal life. And since Christ is omnipresent through the Holy Spirit, he can escort any and all believers at once. Isn't that glorious!

"Now with these promises in view, I propose to you the following sequence of events surrounding the account of Stephens's death that applies to each one of us who has received Christ as Savior and has been regenerated in the spirit. Of course we know this took place with our friend, George.

— Stephen's spirit sensed death was imminent so he looked up into heaven to the Throne Room of God ...

— He sees Jesus standing when He is normally always sitting according to the prophecy in Psalm one-hundred ten. Jesus was standing because He was beginning His descent to come to take Stephen home ...

— Stephen gets an eyeful of Jesus coming for him and everything else is blotted out, including any fear of death. He then swells with courage and cries out, 'Heaven is open! I see the Son of Man standing on the right hand of God!'

— Hearing that gospel stuff,' the unruly throng hauls him out of the city to a secluded place to execute him illegally. By this time Jesus is right nearby ...

— Then while they are throwing the rocks, Jesus walks up to him. Stephen's eyes are now fastened on his Savior as he reaches to him and cries with great expectation, 'Lord Jesus, receive my spirit!' Can't you imagine him saying to himself as he faced his Savior, 'Everything I believed and read about you is true! The promise of Resurrection is standing right before my eyes!'

— Then Stephen kneels down to acknowledge Jesus as his Lord and Master while extending his hand towards Him. 'Lord, lay not this sin to their charge,' he laments just as they embrace. Can you picture in your mind ever having that kind of love and concern for your assassins? 'And when he said this he fell asleep'...

— The stones then take their toll as Stephen's spirit departs with Jesus, leaving a spiritless body to crumple to the ground. Then the final promise is enacted ... Jesus escorts Stephen into glory. They both ascend to heaven together via Jacob's Ladder or Staircase . . . the very same staircase that Jacob saw in Genesis twenty-eight and our brother George Lambert saw on his deathbed. The very same ladder that Jesus escorted both of them to heaven.

Then he ended his sermon.

In his heart, pastor Marcus knew he was led by the Holy Spirit to deliver this sermon. In his heart he also knew that statistics from well-known Christian researchers found that there were over eighty percent of those purporting to be Christians who were attending Christian churches, were in fact, non-believers, and since the day would come for him to give an accounting before Christ, he made sure he presented the gospel and gave invitations to be regenerated as often as the Spirit led him. Today was one of those days.

More than fifteen approached him after he gave the closing benediction. Those who wanted to make sure they would be escorted by Jesus as well. He had to call upon several of his deacons to help out with the altar call.

His son, Jason, gave him another thumb up.

WHEN THE OLD FIRE HORSE HEARS THE BELL

Pastor George sat behind the steering wheel in his car in the First Christian Church parking lot, not mindful that the engine was still running. He was troubled in his spirit and at his age of what he called a youthful 77, and when he thought on what his wife called a senior moment it only made things worse. Her view annoyed him since his last medical checkup showed he was in good physical condition and he believed that extended to his mental faculties as well. He was fine. But he was stuck at this moment on what his wife advised him to do. She wanted him to confront the senior pastor about his recent propensity of indoctrinating liberal theology into his teachings and sermons. Some called this current trend the Christian Left.

He sighed and remembered he asked for the meeting after the last worship service.

His wife Emily, at age 74, being a strong-willed woman and a continuous source of godly wisdom, advised him to speak privately to their senior pastor about this troubling issue; something he was reluctant to do as a pastor emeritus. No, at this time he wasn't having a senior moment, he was simply planning on what to say at the meeting.

He pulled down the sun visor and looked in the mirror. "We have this," he said to himself with a chuckle. Yes, he had several wrinkles on his face along with small bags under his eyes, but he continuously remembered his primary doctor's statement: 'You certainly don't look your age!'

He pushed the sun visor up then blinked several times then shut off the engine. *See, I remembered,* he thought.

In his mind, together with his background in Christian ministry for over forty years, the modern corporate church was under attack and undergoing an enormous upheaval that was indicative of the bible's prophecy on what to expect in the end days before Christ returned—an identity crisis—where there was a great need of godly leadership to bring back the fundamentals of the early church where the inspiration of the Holy Spirit in the Bible was taught from the pulpit and believed by the congregation. This being reflected in their personal lives as a testimony of the fruit of the Spirit to the unbelieving world.

Now, in view of the erosion of biblical values in both the church and society—in his mind—pastors under the guidance of the Holy Spirit, not politicians, are the best spiritual hope to renew America.

He took a deep breath to reinforce his stamina to proceed with his meeting then stepped out of his car and proceeded to the church office. He paused on the sidewalk to survey the church buildings and grounds. *Beautiful,* he thought. Is the expansion of buildings a sign of God's blessings? He wasn't sure. This was a large congregation and by Christian standards, a flagship church with over three thousand enrolled as members promoting various outreaches such as gymnastic workshops, day school for children, international mission trips, and local events to attract the neighbors such as car shows and annual bazaars. Is this the modern version of the Great Commission to go and proclaim the gospel? A puzzled look swept over his face. *Not sure,* he thought. *Not sure.*

* * *

The clerical staff was actively tending to Monday's church business when Pastor George entered the offices. The counting of Sunday's offerings and tallying the attendance records of both Sunday School and worship services along with other various duties were taking place when he arrived. "Good morning, Pastor George!" Wendy, the pastor's secretary said brightly. "So good to see you!"

Pastor George was delighted to be called 'pastor' since that was indeed his title after he was ordained and spent many years in the pulpit, but he often took offence when others in church ministry would avoid calling him 'pastor' as if he was now retired and no longer in that capacity. *Were they being threatened?* He reasoned that when a medical doctor retires, everyone still calls him 'doctor.' It just irked him to see a lack of respect but he was determined to overlook it. "Can I get you a cup of coffee?" Wendy asked.

Pastor George nodded. "That would be nice." He liked Wendy. For a middle-aged woman with three grown children and an unbelieving unemployed husband, she was a sparkling testimony of a Christian who relied upon the Lord for all of her needs. In his mind, she really toughed it out when it came to hardship.

"Pastor Mark will be right with you," Wendy said as she brought him his coffee. "He's meeting with his deacons right now."

Pastor George waved her off. "No problem," he replied and slowly sipped his coffee as he perused the office. Portraits of the current and previous pastors lined the west wall and on the east wall was a mural of Christ hanging on the cross at Calvary. The office was well decorated and reminded him of when he was working at a department store while in seminary and was called into the boss's office for preaching bible prophecy to a fellow worker. The boss's office wall was lined with the previous presidents of the company with his picture elegantly framed at the center. He remembered that the boss—he deliberately forgot his name, warned him not to do any witnessing for God while on company time. He agreed with the premise but announced that he had a higher calling and asked if he could speak to his fellow workers out in the parking lot while on break. His boss wiggled in his seat and said, "I suppose it would be okay."

* * *

Fifteen minutes later the church's seven deacons marched out of the pastor's office. Two of them saluted him as the other four just walked toward the doorway, while one stopped and sat down next to him. "Pastor Mark is in what I call an 'approachable' mood today. So whatever you have to say to him it should go well."

Pastor George tapped his knee. "Thanks Joe. May the Lord honor that prayer," he replied while bobbing his head.

Moments later Pastor Mark came to his office doorway and said to him, "Brother George, come on in. I've been looking forward to meeting with you." Pastor George set his coffee cup down on the end table then stood up while broadcasting a broad smile.

Hopefully you will be happy to see me. May it be so, Pastor George thought and followed his pastor into his office. His office reflected the church's financial worth with leather-bound upholstery, a mahogany desk replete with an iMac computer and a multitude of family pictures. On the wall behind his desk were four framed diplomas and a certificate. The diplomas showed his undergraduate, masters, and his doctorate degree from one of the more prestigious seminaries in America. Next to the laminated degrees was his framed ordination certificate.

Pastor George's observation of Pastor Mark's family at the worship service and fellowship gatherings projected the image that he really had it 'together' when it came to his spiritual, family, and personal qualities and positions. His wife, Linda, was a charming woman who dressed according to the current trends, along with her husband, who displayed jeans under a sport's jacket while preaching on Sunday's, devoid of any neckties or tucked-in shirts, something that was no longer popular in the church.

Pastor George realized that Pastor Mark did indeed have his priorities right. He put obeying the Lord first, leading his family next, and the guiding of the church family to follow, his hobbies and playtime last. *Good stuff,* he thought. In his mind, this should be an indication of his willingness to hear constructive criticism relative to ministry for the betterment of the glory of God. *May it be so.*

Together with his fortitude and ambition Pastor George determined to persuade his senior pastor that he personally enjoyed his relationship with his God and that his purpose in life was to spread the magnetic character of Christ to others for the benefit of the church.

Pastor Mark pointed to the cushioned chair next to his desk [the chair used by anyone who came for counseling] and said calmly as he stood next to one of his bookcases, "How are things going with you? You and Emily okay?"

Pastor George nodded and then said with a brief voice, "Emily and I are fine and thought I should have a talk with you about some of our concerns regarding current church issues."

Pastor Mark bit his lower lip then nodded with a facial expression of concern as if expecting some kind of rebuke. "Like what?" he replied then pulled out his chair then sat down and picked up his notepad.

Pastor George wiggled in his seat. "I am hoping that my experience as a pastor and the wisdom of longevity will be of service to you as I express my thoughts pertaining to ministry. Truthfully Pastor Mark I think our church is becoming an event church. If you look back over the past few months, every weekend has a different event going on. While each one may have value, where is the emphasis on the Word of God? I might be considered an old fire horse but my experience in the pulpit has shown me change only takes place by hearing more of God's word and believing it! In my belief, God never intended a pastor's work to be a human effort and that he implanted in humans the ability to make sense of life and in your particular case, you have demonstrated that you experienced a calling from God to shepherd this flock and that your pastoring here is not just a career move—"

He received an approving nod from pastor Mark.

"Go on!" Pastor Mark insisted and cracked a smile as if the worst was over.

"—I believe you have demonstrated that it is not essential that you be happy—although I see the joy of the Lord in your face which is exclusive of positive events—but that you matter and that you're making a difference here at First Christian. Because you are *called*, you will be ... " he paused and shot his eyes up to heaven for approval, " ... you will be *stretched*. Unlike the corporate world where the CEO's are often stretched to make command decisions before their board for approval, you make command decisions and pray for God's approval ... " he paused, " ... right?"

"Of course!" Pastor Mark replied and took a deep breath. "That's our philosophy of ministry here and I aim to set a godly example, and I pray my stewardship to the congregation has proven that." He frowned. "Let me amend my answer. My real method is that I pray about an issue, then seek God's direction and approval and then implement the decision."

Pastor George nodded. "Good call," he said in agreement.

"Okay, so what's really on your mind George?" Pastor Mark asked inquisitively. "I have the gut feeling you're leading up to putting out what you see as a potential fire here in the church."

"That's providential that you should say that," Pastor George replied with a chortle. "I do see myself as an old fire horse that hears the bell and immediately is ready to respond. One of my concerns is the use of the word *story*. In my tenure as a pastor, I never heard the word of God being referred to as a *story*. But now it seems that's all I hear. 'Continuing on with the story,' or 'we will be studying today the story of—.' I hope you understand how that can be misunderstood—a story can be true or made up. A doubt is present as to the authenticity of what you are trying to communicate.

"In my way of thinking the fire alarm bell of the corporate church's condition has sounded and in the mind of Pastor Chuck Swindol, 'there is no retirement for pastors.' As long as we're alive, we serve as pastors whether active or retired.

"In point of fact, men, women, and pastors are living longer now and many churches have a high percentage of retired-inactive pastors in their congregation." He pulled out his cell phone and read aloud a passage from his notes. "Pastor John C. Maxwell describes a congregation that is led by a genuine pastor-leader: 'Morale is high. Turnover is low. Needs are being met. Goals are behind realized . . . Leading and influencing others is fun. Problems are solved with minimum effort. Fresh statistics are shared on regular basis with the people that undergird the growth of the organization.'"

"I appreciate your viewpoint," Pastor Mark said as his body language signaled discomfort. "So what is your recommendation?"

"I have a passion for serving God as part of my unique calling and if that means suggesting that we put salt in the congregation's oats to heighten their thirst for God's Word, then I want to be a part of that."

"Interesting. Well, I do attend a monthly prayer meeting with other pastors of our denomination in our region and from my perspective," pastor Mark explained, "they're very content with the way things are and do not voice any disgruntlement."

"Does that mean that they are satisfied with the tolerance doctrine that encourages abortion approval, sexual deviation, worship music that sounds like a rock concert, and supporting those nations and colleges that are anti-Israel?" Pastor George probed. "Somehow they forget that Jesus was a Jew and that God's promise is to protect them."

Pastor Mark fidgeted slightly. "I do see a metamorphous taking place. This is true. In many churches they are catering to the millennials and accordingly phasing out the old form of worship—including the traditional hymns and reading only from the King James version of the bible, etc." he replied as if making a concession. "But we who are in ministry leadership believe this trend is for the betterment of the corporate church. If that means adding 'fun events' to attract the neighbors, then that's good. As far as Israel is concerned many pastors boarder on their doctrines and many believe in replacement theology where the promises to Israel no longer are in effect but that they extend to the corporate church because the Jews rejected their messiah."

Pastor George was familiar with replacement theology and did not believe it to be the accurate rendering of scripture since God's unconditional covenant with David was irrevocably in place. In fact, due to Israel's blindness to Jesus salvation was extended to the gentiles. *Reason with him*, his inner voice dictated. "Pastor, I want to come alongside you as a biblical 'sage,' like the sages who advised the kings and high priests in the Old Testament. One who can offer encouragement, one who can offer the voices he hears coming from the flock that may be approving or detrimental to your leadership. In no way do I purpose to threaten you or your deacons."

"This sounds like you're looking for a revival," Pastor Mark noted, "but I don't see the need. I believe 'we're just fine.'"

"Pastor Mark, your next appointment is here," they heard from Wendy over the office intercom.

Pastor George took the cue from God's Spirit. He stood up and said calmly, "It was really great to talk to you pastor Mark, and I'm believing you took our discussion as a 'love' message from an old fire horse that is listening for the bell to sound so that I can ride with you on the hook and ladder truck."

Pastor Mark stood up and walked to pastor George, put his arm around his shoulder and said, "I will review our discussion with my deacons." He then walked him to the door and waved to the next member waiting to see him. "God bless, George," he ended with a tender repetitive slap on his back.

* * *

His coffee and biscotti along with his wife were waiting for him in the kitchen when he got home. He pledged to himself that he would give a good report about his meeting with the pastor. "So, how did it go?" Emily asked as she pointed to the kitchen table.

Emily had the memory of a 500-gigawatt hard drive. Events and discussions, even facial expressions that occurred in their family over their fifty-year marriage were indelibly etched in her mind. There was no getting around it or befuddling her when it came to past events. Accordingly he had to give her a clear report. "To be honest," he began with a shake of the head, "not sure. We talked about the issues you and I discussed beforehand, but I'm not sure he received our talk in the spirit it was intended. I suspect he viewed me as being a little hostile and old fashioned since we talked about things him and his deacons do not talk about."

She poured the coffee and handed him his biscotti with a napkin. "So what you're telling me is that he didn't see you as an agent of reconciliation. Right?"

"Not sure."

"Did you talk to him about his use of the word 'story' when he addresses the inspired scriptures as if it could very well be fiction not documented fact?" Emily asked.

"Yes. I tried to display godly wisdom and ministry experience as counsel to serve as a formula for fulfillment as well as a balance for his leadership as the senior pastor and come across with advice for needed change, not novel ideas. I don't want to come across as a critic or enemy but as a helpmate so to speak as—" he paused then added, "—an old fire horse that hears the bell and wants to join in putting out fires."

His wife had the spiritual discernment of a prophet and believed he did the best he could, after all, she reasoned, he is not on staff, over the age of 70, and viewed by the younger generation as being an old 'fuddy,' unimaginative, and ultra conservative—not willing to adopt to the modern world. "Okay, so we will leave this whole project of your talk with the pastor on the altar before God and let him work it out."

"Good advice," Pastor George replied after taking another sip of his coffee. "And if there is a leading for us to relocate—we will pray for God's guidance—but at this point I am prepared to stay here even if there is no change simply because in the process of time our influence may bring about godly modifications."

* * *

The next Sunday, when Pastor George and Emily sat in their favorite pew in the sanctuary for the worship service they were expecting to have a special time of hearing God's word and entering into a personal time with Jesus, but the strobe lights were active as the music ministry belted out the current favorite hymns by contemporary Christian artists.

Pastor George glanced at Emily and then shrugged his shoulders. *You left the problem with God, remember?* he reminded himself. She grabbed hold of his hand and squeezed it. He knew she agreed with him.

After the worship period and the announcements where broadcast, pastor Mark ascended the platform and then stood behind the pulpit. He opened his Bible then shot a look at pastor George and said, "Today we are going to hear God's story of trusting him from the Book of Daniel . . . "

OUR DEFENCE MECHANISM

OCEANSIDE CHRISTIAN CHURCH, OCEANSIDE, FLORIDA

P astor Nick grew increasingly agitated as he read about the condescending faction of the corporate church called Modern Christianity. The Internet report troubled him because the emerging movement with their leftist theology and ideology was gaining momentum within the liberal branch of Christianity with the ultimate goal of infiltrating the conservative platform under the guise of religious unity. Even though he was in his late fifties, he believed he was up to speed on the issues that threatened the church that came from both society as well as the liberal seminaries.

In his mind he saw this movement as the advance of apostasy that is recurrent throughout the history of the church but in his thinking Modern Christianity has taken a quantum leap into what is defined in the book of Jude as an indication of the last days. This threat is deliberately placed by the Holy Spirit prior to the book of Revelation for a reason. This movement will precipitate the rise of the reign of the Antichrist. Yes, he was worried. He had to talk to another pastor about his concerns.

* * *

JACKSONVILLE CHRISTIAN CHURCH ASSOCIATION

At the next pastor's monthly luncheon Pastor Nick deliberately sat next to a fellow pastor who he believed also held to his conservative doctrines and values. But he had doubts, knowing that doubt is the devil's darkroom where he produces negatives. He wasn't sure of his fellow pastor's convictions when it came to newer movements that has besieged the corporate church and caused many to capitulate under the new thinking in order to preserve their church membership. He would test the waters.

"Pastors," the chairman announced to the fifteen pastors, "today we will have our lunch first then discuss our latest addition to our pastor's administration study library, *The Strength You Need* by Robert Morgan."

The chairman, Pastor Josh, did a great job of motivating the group to rely on the Lord for the strength needed to combat the devil and his attack on the church as well as attacking the pastor's personal life. The pastors were encouraged and determined to press on. Pastor Nick saw the godly response as affirmation that he should approach his fellow pastor, Ron, who he believed had a kindred spirit.

As the meeting starting to break up pastor Nick tapped pastor Ron on his shoulder and asked as he pointed to a corner of the meeting room, "Can we talk for few minutes about our ministry?"

"Of course," Pastor Ron answered and followed him. Pastor Ron was a middle-aged pastor with over twenty years as a lead pastor with a wife firmly committed to supporting him along with two teenage girls still in high school. A prime candidate in pastor Nick's mind. But then again, he had his doubts about the infiltration of perverted doctrines that many pastors were deceived into adopting.

"I've been doing some research on the current movement within the corporate church called *Modern Christianity*—" he dropped his voice, "—have you heard about this?"

"*Modern Christianity*? No," Pastor Ron replied. "I haven't heard the name, but I have been getting some strange emails encouraging me to visit some websites that are offering suggestions on how to attract more of the public to my church," he replied somewhat pensively. "What's going on?"

"Well, I believe the corporate church is being threatened by new theology from *Modern Christianity* that has its foundation in Marxism and Socialism," he explained. "In fact just recently there was a march by the Revolutionary Communists of America (RCA) in Philadelphia by 300 demonstrators chanting, 'class war' and 'fight the rich and feed the poor.' They are committed to the complete overthrow of capitalism. This is an enemy working on the outside that will in the end exterminate Christianity.

"Yes, this is an attack against our democracy that threatens the church from the outside, but there are other enemies that are attacking from the inside," he continued. "I have formulated an analogy. I believe we have woodpeckers like Atheists, Agnostics, the RCA, the LGBTQ and others that threaten the church tree from the outside while there are carpenter ants like *Modern Christianity* that threaten the church tree from the inside. They are concealed until the internal structural damage brings the tree down—" he paused then shook his head and added, "—unless we conservatives see the 'sawdust' at the base of the tree caused by the carpenter ants—or we as conservatives recognize the infiltration of apostate doctrine into the church and act accordingly, for sure the church will fall down."

Pastor Ron grew pensive. "This is not good," he replied. "Let me look further into this and get back to you," he promised.

"I appreciate your commitment and look toward hearing from you," Pastor Nick replied then hugged his fellow pastor and drove back to his church.

* * *

Pastor Nick was both deeply troubled and intrigued that such a movement like *Modern Christianity* could creep into the corporate church unnoticed and secretly promote apostasy, antisemitism, gradual godlessness, as well as advancing socialism. He marveled. Where are the watchmen on the wall who are to warn the church of the subversive nature of these so-called modern movements that are already attacking? He needed to do more research before forming any kind of force to combat this seditious faction within the church. But first he had to check a passage in the Bible that underscored and supported his thinking. He found it in the book of Romans.

> Now I urge you, brethren, note those who cause divisions and offenses, contrary to the doctrine which you learned, and avoid them. For those who are such do not serve our Lord Jesus Christ, but their own belly, and by smooth words and flattering speech deceive the hearts of the simple. (Romans 16:17-18)

Yeah, he thought, *this is happening before my very eyes.* The clause that stuck in his craw was: 'contrary to the doctrine which you learned.' He would dig into the doctrine of *Modern Christianity* to compare it with

Paul's teaching then assemble his task force of fundamentalists as watchmen to warn the church.

At first he discovered that the contemporary church was vulnerable to apostasy because churchgoers had become apathetic and doctrinal tolerance has set in allowing the acceptance of false dogmas. He remembered a portion of the Bible that reinforced his research in John chapter six where many disciples of Christ turned away from him after he gave the parable of the bread of life and explained this divine mystery that applied to himself. When pastor Nick thought on it he again recognized that those who turned away said 'This is a hard saying; who can understand this?' But they were really 'followers,' or apostates, not apostles or believers.

Checking the Internet on a variety of Christian churches in America he recognized that many of those he labeled *Modern Christianity* offered their support of illegal immigration, Marxists organizations, and same-sex marriage in an attempt to accommodate visitors in new and exciting ways.

This branch of apostate Christianity took steps to bring in more people to the sanctuary. These steps included the replacing of pews with theater-like chairs along with sermons that were diluted and shortened; Bible readings were abbreviated and traditional hymns, organs, and choirs were replaced with rock-and-roll songs with a smidgeon of God backed up with different sounding guitars. These steps were designed to make the church more attractive to seekers and unbelievers. Yes, he discovered, there was a huge public response since the subject matter from the pulpit went from turning from sin, repentance, and regeneration to 'feed the poor' and be 'seeker friendly.' The Bible was no longer an authoritative voice in the church and in the life of the churchgoer but merely the story that may or may not be true, depending on your point of view. Instead of the reading of the Bible being a narrative rendering by the Holy Spirit, the Bible has become a 'story' like one of Aesop's fables.

Pastor Nick pushed back from his desk after his hour of research to fetch himself a cup of coffee then decided he would confer with his friend pastor Ron to discuss his findings and to get another pastor's point of view.

* * *

SALVATION CHRISTIAN CHURCH

Receiving the invite to meet pastor Ron at his church to discuss his investigation on *Modern Christianity* pleased pastor Nick and came somewhat as a surprise. For some reason, and maybe it was his intuition, he thought he would be the one to initiate the follow up invitation to explore the matter. *We'll see*, he thought.

Pastor Ron's church, the Salvation Christian Church, was not a flagship church in his denomination but was amply attended by the residents in neighboring towns. He had over one thousand members. Before going to meet him pastor Nick noticed on his website that the church boasted about their goal to move toward the universal one-world church. A movement he disagreed with since he believed the Bible was against universalism and ecumenicalism that taught that all people would experience some sort of divine salvation after they die. That includes non-Christian faiths like Islam, Buddhism, and Hinduism.

The outside of the church was not overly ostentatious but did possess several indicators on the church sign that seemed to indicate their liberal stance toward politics, the nation of Israel, and family issues. *Definitely appealing to the masses*, Pastor Nick thought. *But maybe I'm reading into it too deeply. We'll see.*

Pastor Ron greeted him warmly as he stood at the entrance to his office. "Been very busy," he opened with, "but never too busy to meet with a fellow pastor." Then he motioned for pastor Nick to take a cushioned seat opposite his desk then said, "I've had an opportunity amidst my active schedule to look into *Modern Christianity* and I wanted to discuss it with you before I take action on it."

"That's good," Pastor Nick replied anxiously. "On my part, I've decided to call our defensive movement, *Our Defense Mechanism*. The meaning being that we want to defend our sister churches against the liberal and subversive *Modern Christianity* for taking the aggressive steps to undermine and destroy everything we believe in and hold dear. We need to combat their progression! This really is becoming a war."

Pastor Ron simply nodded and grew thoughtful. He appeared to observe, take note of, and to prepare to defend his differing viewpoint. "I'm trying to balance what I've read on this subject together with your take on the matter along with what my deacons and congregation believe is best for them and our visitors," he said with eyes pleading for understanding.

Pastor Nick sensed his duplicity. "But pastor Ron, surely you read that the philosophy of ministry of this movement is a form of doctrinal variance, rooted in gnostic thinking and places humanistic and logical reasoning above the Bible's position on the way we live according to scriptural doctrines, morality and justice.

"This progressive movement follows its own theological ponderings and denies the basic truths such as Creationism, regeneration, and the imputation of sin from Adam." He grew increasingly concerned. "Can't you see the deeper implications this modern apostasy has on the well-being of the whole conservative church?"

"Well, I'm not convicted that this is the way to go," Pastor Ron replied. "I believe that it doesn't matter how our church views this movement—even if we don't see that it aligns perfectly with the Bible," he argued. "I mean in today's world we must be open to adjust our take on the Bible in order to win people over to God. We need to be tolerant."

Pastor Nick simply looked at him in disbelief. "So you're saying that you agree with their rendering of ministry that doesn't address the basics of our faith? You realize that they—according to the reports I read Online—never discuss the fundamental issues of evangelism, regeneration, discipleship, or Christ's Second Coming? Their attitude is that they want the church members to feel comfortable when at worship and Bible study."

Pastor Ron rolled his eyes. "I'm of the persuasion as they say to 'wait and see.' In other words, I'm not saying I disagree with your protective stance of the church, but I'm not going to judge this new movement now.

"Remember, in the first century church there were many disputes over the 'new thinking' and 'new doctrines' of who Christ is, and I tend to see this in the same light," Pastor Ron explained. "Things will straighten out by themselves."

Pastor Nick sat looking at him, his expression enigmatic. He was getting the picture that his fellow pastor was not convinced of the danger that the corporate church was facing internal corruption as well as external corruption and unwilling to stand against it. He wanted to stay in his own comfort zone. He stood up and extended his hand. "I see where you're coming from and even though I disagree with your assessment, I pray you will continue to investigate *Modern Christianity* and if your sentiments change—" he paused to carefully chose his words, "—you will consider joining our defensive movement."

"We will see how things unfold," Pastor Ron said blandly.

Pastor Nick gave him a brotherly hug and left.
He was greatly disappointed.

* * *

JACKSONVILLE CHRISTIAN CHURCH ASSOCIATION

Pastor Nick had great respect for Pastor Josh, the middle-aged chairman of the Jacksonville Christian Church Association. He had a volume of experience regarding church politics and administration as well as initiating start-up churches. It was him who he would go to at the first sign of conflict be it in his own heart or the heart of his church at Oceanside. He was the next thing to a prayer partner.

His office was located in a converted industrial condo that provided ample room for both staff offices as well as a conference room that often served as the location for the monthly pastoral fellowship luncheons and teaching episodes. Even though pastor Josh had a hectic schedule, he made time for his fellow pastor to discuss what he conveyed to him was an urgent matter.

"So my friend, what's this concern of yours all about?" Pastor Josh asked after giving him a godly hug then directed him into his office and pointed to a seat near his desk.

"I'm coming to you not only in the form of a prayer partner and fellow pastor, but today as a mentor. I need help to ascertain what direction I should go in with what I call a quantum leap in apostasy that has befallen today's church. It's called *Modern Christianity*."

Pastor Josh nodded. "I've heard about it but haven't explored it. Is it a threat to the church?"

"Oh, it's a threat alright," Pastor Nick replied as a muscle jerked in his right cheek. "A big threat."

Pastor Josh took out his notepad. "Okay, give me the short version as to why it's a threat."

With his voice vibrating with intensity he said, "To begin with, let me ask that if you agree with this being a threat that you will reach out to the other pastors in our association to inform them?"

"Yes, if I agree that it's a threat."

"Well the reason I am qualifying this is because I already attempted to recruit another pastor in our association into this defense mechanism against this rising apostasy, but he couldn't decide nor could his deacon board," Pastor Nick explained. "I call my movement '*Our Defense Mechanism*' because we need to *defend* our churches from this Satanic adversary with the truth of God's Word."

"Okay, agreed. If what you say is so—I'll help you spread it out into the churches."

Pastor Nick knew within himself that this movement was evil. He shot a prayer up to God asking for divine prudence. "My spirit testified that this new wave of theology was planned to wash away the fundamental precepts of our faith. To begin with this movement questions whether there is sin at all or if it was a manmade concept. Then it applies this thinking to foster a blanket of forgiveness to homosexual behavior and gay marriages, abortion, and premarital sex. They label this evil as a social progression that cannot be helped.

"Further, those who espouse *Modern Christianity* principles believe their personal freedoms are a matter of personal preferences that includes their right to full-term abortion, gender change, the ignoring of the rule of law that leads to open borders and to public rebellion and demonstrations exemplified in the dispute over Israel's God-given land verses Palestinian ownership. Yet we know that all of these dictates and changes come under the umbrella of God's sovereignty and that He is allowing all of this to bring humanity to their knees and plead with God for his intervention.

"In sum, the goal of this atheistic movement is to win over the corporate church into morally accepting the anti-family agenda of homosexuality, transgenderism, pedophilia and any form of sexual deviance occurring today. The way I see it is that this tactic is indeed gaining traction in today's church and the hierarchy in the Christian church must decide if it is willing to compromise its foundational truths and cave into their theology or stand firm on our faith and fight against the movement—" he suddenly paused. "What say you?"

Pastor Josh was pensive as he thought on pastor Nick's assessment and commentary then reached over to his desktop books and pulled out a book detailing the life of the early evangelist Charles Finney. "Listen to this," he said and began to quote a page from the text:

> "'Brethren, our preaching will bear its legitimate fruits. If immorality prevails in the land, the fault is ours in a great degree. If there is a decay of conscience, the pulpit is responsible for it. If the church is degenerate and worldly, the pulpit is responsible for it. If

Satan rules in our halls of legislation the pulpit is responsible for it. Let us not ignore this fact, my dear brethren; but let us lay it to heart and be thoroughly awake to our responsibility in respect to the morals of this nation.'"

Pastor Josh replaced the book on his desk then said after hesitating fractionally, "The problem in getting great things from God is holding on for the last half hour. Truthfully, I don't know who first quoted that, but I believe we are in the last half hour before Jesus returns. So for my part, I will endorse your fight against *Modern Christianity*."

"I know it's a risk," Pastor Nick replied, but as you did, I'll give you a quote." He pulled out his cell phone and opened the iCloud app and then went to his quotes: "'We are paralyzed by fear of taking risks. Behold the turtle—he makes progress only when he sticks his neck out.' Quoted by Bryant Conant, distinguished president of Harvard."

"Excellent application," Pastor Josh said, nodding and approving.

"Well, with your permission I will put together my deacons to adopt a summary and statement of these insidious apostate creeds and form a task force or campaign to reach out into our church network to warn them. I am going to implore the long arm of God to reach down and throttle this evil."

Pastor Josh escorted him to his office doorway then hugged him. "Go with the King today and be a blessing."

Pastor Nick was overly joyful now that he had an ally in leadership to help him in his fight.

* * *

OCEANSIDE CHRISTIAN CHURCH, OCEANSIDE, FLORIDA

Pastor Nick asked his wife, Lynn, and several women from his church to prepare coffee and donuts for his deacons before engaging them in the project of preparing and sending out snail-mail letters to the leadership of the association churches. He decided that the email letters often did not convey the sanctity, passion, and emotion that regular mail did so, even though it was an arduous task and more costly, he believed it would bear more fruit.

"Remember brothers," pastor Nick began after he openly prayed for their mission success, "this is our first step to warn the churches of the corruption besetting them. We have the backing of the association director so we will confront this adversary full throttle until they are defeated. If we must, we will all go door-to-door with our petitions to arrest the advance of the enemy." From there he rehearsed the letter he had prepared for them to send out. "In short, this letter after my salutation explains that our churches are being attacked in the fashion the book of Jude prophesizes. I explain that false doctrines are disguised as societal advancements and that tolerance is the central theme for today's churches in order to experience growth.

"We are asking our fellow churches to carefully examine any notion of changing their conservative doctrines under the scrutiny of the Holy Spirit, not the vote of the congregational sheep who are often led astray from the truth by the liberal media or their own foolish interpretations of the Bible."

All his deacons, along with the ladies that were helping out raised their hands in praise after he completed his summary of his letter. Then one of the deacon's wives shouted out, "May this letter act like one of Paul's letters to the churches and bring them back to Jesus!"

"May it be so!" Pastor Nick yelled back.

* * *

JACKSONVILLE CHRISTIAN CHURCH ASSOCIATION

"I called you in, pastor Nick, because I received a phone call from a fellow pastor who objects to your attack against *Modern Christianity*," Pastor Josh began. "He said he met with you and that you 'knocked heads' regarding your steadfast position to warn the churches of this movement. He thought you were narrow-minded and that your title of '*Our Defense Mechanism*' was much too rough and needed to be toned down. He added that you disagreed with him because you sensed his—as he called it, his 'neutrality'—and that he's now on you enemy list."

Destruction must give way to construction, Pastor Nick thought. He wiggled in his seat. "Yes, I can see that he would interpret our meeting in that light if he were predisposed to reject any change in his ministry that might result in some form of conflict and result in a loss of membership that would have a direct impact on their finances," he replied with a tinge of sarcasm. "However, I believe you agree with me and can see that our nation has gone from ordered liberty and unparalleled prosperity to the godless, sin-reveling culture we are witnessing today and that it is evident in the violence and lawlessness infecting every facet of our society. While at one time we were 'America the Beautiful' we have become the America on a trajectory toward destruction with our leaders celebrating wickedness throughout the land.

"With biblical foundations being rejected wholesale throughout Christianity, the church needs to repent and return to God before His patience is exhausted and pours out judgment on us—" he paused then raised his hands in the air. "Doesn't anybody see what's happening?"

"I agree with you, but my hands are tied," Pastor Josh replied with his hands clenched into fists at his sides as a demonstration. "Malevolent ideologies, cults, foreign agents, and illegals are rushing in to fill the ensuing vacuum caused by 'neutral' Christianity." He stopped speaking, stood up then pulled a folding chair next to pastor Nick. "I will continue to pray for your movement, pastor, to defend God's Word and when the other pastors come to our monthly meeting I will give you the floor to address them face-to-face. But until then I can only pray that God in his mercy will slow this movement and finally extinguish it before it's too late."

"I could not ask for more," Pastor Nick replied then added kindly, "In the unforgiving calculus of life, my prayer is that divine intervention and mercy would occur before judgment sets in."

* * *

OCEANSIDE CHRISTIAN CHURCH, OCEANSIDE, FLORIDA

Pastor Nick rehearsed his proposed Sunday worship service announcement to his wife after breakfast to get her approval. She was uncomfortable fearing in-house reprisals but was convicted that he was directed by the Holy Spirit to warn his flock of the radical movement and beg them to pray for the corporate church's repentance to ward off the attack before God's judgment set in to punish the church for its laxity.

The congregation received warmly his 'Our Defense Mechanism' approach to dismantle Modern Christianity's plot to destroy the corporate church, vowing to support in any way they could. But the support from the association churches was minimal and disappointing.

After two months of campaigning, phone calls, visits to neighboring churches, discussions at the monthly meetings with other pastors, the reaction was mostly pushback.

THE CHURCH WEDDING

T *oday is going to be a special day for us*, Cindy said to herself as she set the dinner table that included two low-light candles, her best silverware and her ceramic chinaware all on her mom's finest linen tablecloth. Topping off the special offering she included Bernie's favorite wine.

Bernie is a thirty-one-year-old structural engineer who lives life on schedule. Knowing this, Cindy lit the candles at exactly five-fifteen then proceeded to play their romantic oldies on her XM radio. *She was all set.*

Bernie walked into his condo, shot a look into the vestibule mirror to remind himself how compact and sinewy he was then suddenly turned and realized Cindy was in the kitchen doorway in his favorite nightgown signaling him to join her. He smiled then whispered in wonder, "Wow, what's going on?"

"Today's going to be a special day for us," she replied with fluttering eyes.

Bernie sized her petite body up and down then replied, "I'm with you! You're my main squeeze! What did you have in mind?"

Cindy put her right index finger to her lips. "Shush! Not until after dinner!"

Bernie nodded then followed her to the dinner table and noticed the bottle of his favored wine. "I have a feeling I'm going to be persuaded to buy something terribly expensive," he said as if he should expect a huge demand but then dismissed it as simply a romantic outreach.

It was after dinner, dessert and coffee, and their intimate time in the bedroom that the big question would be asked.

"Okay, so now that you've appeased 'the savage beast,' in me what's this all about?" Bernie asked with an inquisitive smile.

Cindy's stomach tightened. "I want to get married!" she exclaimed. "We've been together for five years and I love you and want to make it legal and then I want to have children." In her mind, being a size six with long black flowing hair and a vibrant personality, a sharp intellect that qualified her as medical office receptionist, he would realize she was really a great catch and readily agree.

"Uh-huh," Bernie replied, eyes narrowing.

Silence.

In his thinking he had to keep her off the market seeing that he believed her to be gorgeous. "Okay, so we'll go to a Justice of the Peace and get married," his voice was lower, conspiratorial.

"Bernie, I want to have a church wedding—to make it official before God—to get his blessing—not just to satisfy our friends, family or the public!" Cindy argued sharply.

Bernie spun around. "But we haven't been in a church since we've been together."

"It's my bad," she replied sheepishly then explained, "I've been a Christian since I went to church with my parents when I was a child, but I haven't really been practicing and didn't want to get into a discussion or argument with you over the subject.

"I know that at one time you were a churchgoer, so don't you agree that we want to have God in our lives—especially if we are going to have a family so that our children get religion?"

He threw his hands up in the air in a gesture of surrender. In his mind, and experience dictated, it would be her way or no way. "Fine," he replied to mollify her. "Set it up."

* * *

MEADOWBROOK CHRISTIAN CHURCH

While Cindy sat in the outer office of the non-denominational church waiting to meet with the pastor, his secretary walked to her and handed her their two-page church policy document on weddings. "Pastor Warren will be with you shortly, but in the meantime, please review our church policy agreement," she said with a broad smile and returned to her office.

When Cindy first skimmed the church policy agreement on weddings she was slightly overwhelmed thinking that there were many requirements in order for the pastor to perform the wedding ceremony at this church. At further review she noted that the church would only allow an ordained, licensed pastor to perform the ceremony. Marriages shall only be between a man and a woman; other pastors performing marriages at Meadowbrook Christian Church may only perform marriages between a man and a woman. All marriages conducted at Meadowbrook must undergo pre-marital counseling [this also qualifies the couple requesting licensures through the state for a discount]. All of their Scriptural texts would be from the King James or New International Bibles.

The remainder of the document instructed the applicant on the member and non-member prices for the use of facilities and general rules regarding the care and use of church property. Then there was a signature line for the applicant. Cindy thought about it and wondered what the pre-marital counseling would be all about.

Moments later the pastor walked out of his office up to Cindy then said as he extended his hand, "Hi, I'm Pastor Warren. It's nice to meet you. Kindly come into my office so we can talk."

Cindy returned the handshake. "Thank you," she said and smiled luminously while following him.

"My secretary, Jenny, said you would like to be married here at Meadowbrook. So tell me a little about you and your partner that brings you here," he asked as he led her to a chair in front of his desk.

Cindy noticed Pastor Warren appeared to be in his mid 40s with slight balding and a black and white cropped short beard. He wore jeans and a shirt and tie with the shirt sleeves rolled up. He appeared to be a proactive pastor. "Well, I—" she paused to choose her words carefully. "—I would like to have God's blessing on my relationship with my boyfriend by getting married in a church," she began. "Then I would like to start a family.

"My boyfriend, Bernie, has a good career as a structural engineer and I'm a medical receptionist so we are set financially—"

Suddenly Pastor Warren waved her off. 'That's nice, but I'm more interested in both you and Bernie's spiritual relationship with Jesus so let's start there," he said trenchantly.

Cindy wiggled in her seat. She was becoming increasingly uncomfortable. "Well, we've been living together for the past five years and at this time of my life I would like to make it—" she paused and then added with quotation marks in the air, 'official' before God and country."

"We at Meadowbrook would certainly like to accommodate you," Pastor Warren began cordially. "Before we get into the specifics let me explain what our concept of marriage is. Marriage is a union ordained by God. For Christians, marriage is a covenant through which a man and a woman are called to live together before God with lives that honor the Bible. Marriage was first instituted by God in the early chapters of Genesis, codified in the Levitical law; the Old Testament prophets compared it to a relationship between God and his people.

"Jesus explained the original intention and core elements of marriage, and several New Testament Epistles give explicit instructions on this union. Marriage is a typology of Christ and the Church and as such we here at Meadowbrook view marriage as a profound spiritual institution established by God." After the explanation he stared at her. "Are you okay with this definition?"

Cindy fidgeted slightly. *I had no idea this would be so involved*, she thought. "I guess—"

Pastor Warren interpreted her answer to mean he should probe deeper. "This would come out in our pre-marriage counseling, but for now, can you describe your relationship with Jesus and that of your fiancé?"

Cindy's breath caught in her throat and she hesitated for a few seconds. "Um, well, I went to public schools then to vacation Bible school when in my teens and decided to follow God after that but when I went to college I sort of got away from it."

Her explanation troubled him. Over the years that he's been in the pastorate, if there was any evidence of a person being truly regenerated in the Spirit it is exhibited in their love for God's Word, a passion for the lost, and a changed life. This reformation does not take years and is continuous throughout our lives. For the Holy Spirit to take a hiatus for many years was inconsistent with the Bible's doctrine on being born again. He needed more info. Marriages may be made in heaven, he thought, but they have to be worked out on earth.

"And what about Bernie?"

Cindy registered the look on Pastor Warren's face. She sighed and explained, "Well, truthfully, his first response to getting married was that we should just have a civil marriage to make it legal. He's not very religious and doesn't like going to church."

Pastor Warren hesitated fractionally to compose his thoughts. "Well you read our wedding policy and noticed that we require pre-marital counseling so set that up with my Jenny and we'll work from there."

"Thanks very much, pastor," Cindy replied as she stood up to leave.

"Hold on," Pastor Warren said as he reached for her hand. "Let's just have a word of prayer before you go."

Cindy nodded and prayed with him then set out to make the pre-marriage counseling appointment after signing the church policy agreement.

* * *

When Bernie returned home from work he was hoping his greeting would be the same as the night before, but it was not. Cindy was wearing a jogging outfit and appeared upset. "What's with you?" he asked the moment he set his eyes on her. "Everything okay?"

She handed him his glass of wine then directed him to their sofa. "I went to see the pastor of Meadowbrook today and—" she hesitated, deep in thought as to how to present this conundrum to him. Seconds past then she took a deep breath then added, "In order for us to get married in this church we need to have pre-marital counseling."

"I figured as much," he complained. Then he stared at her in helpless frustration and nodded gloomily. "Let's just go to another church where their rules are different. And if that's a problem, let's just skip it altogether. I mean after all, it's no big deal these days to live together. That's why most of our friends are doing it without the bother of all the red tape involved in getting married."

"But Bernie, I want a church wedding!" she argued passionately. "I want to invite my family, our friends, and even many of our co-workers to celebrate our love relationship and the starting of a family." She sat next to him and said in a soothing voice, "Besides, what's wrong with the pre-marital counseling? We don't have anything to be ashamed of, right?"

Bernie did an immediate internal assessment and knew he would lose the fight. "You feel comfortable with this guy—this pastor?" he asked curiously. "We can really feel relaxed with him?"

The tension wilted. "Yes, I do."

"Okay, set it up."

* * *

MEADOWBROOK CHRISTIAN CHURCH

Cindy fiddled with her purse strings then repeatedly rechecked the news and messages on her cell phone as she waited for Bernie to arrive so they could see Pastor Warren. "Cup of coffee and donut?" his secretary, Jenny, asked in an attempt to lessen her anxiety that was very perceptible.

"No, I'm good," she replied as her shoulders rose and fell.

Jenny checked Pastor Warren's afternoon schedule on her iMac then said, "Will your fiancé, Bernie, be joining you?"

"Yes, he's on his way," Cindy replied. "I just texted him. He had to take half a day off from work to attend so he should be here within the next ten minutes."

"Fine," Jenny said with a smile then walked into the pastor's office to update him.

Actually it was thirty minutes until Bernie arrived.

Bernie walked into the church office and gave it a quick visual scan then spotted Cindy and sat down next to her and asked in a somber tone, "Everything okay? You look a little nervous."

Cindy stiffened slightly. "You're late!"

"Couldn't help it—there was some kind of political rally blocking the traffic on the main road to here—really slowed me down," he explained.

She reached over and clutched his hand. "Okay, fine. Just be nice to the pastor," she advised.

"Oh, I will," he replied. "What's his name again?"

"Pastor Warren," she replied with a tolerant smile.

Moments later Jenny answered her desk phone. "Pastor Warren will see you both now," she said then escorted them to his doorway.

As they walked in Pastor Warren was returning to his bookshelf the book he often referred to, *The Christian Counselor's Manual* by Jay Adams. "Nice to see you again, Cindy," he said then extended his hand to Bernie. "I'm Warren. I welcome you to our church."

Bernie immediately felt at ease. Later he would try to explain how it happened, but to his surprise the apprehension he was experiencing just evaporated. "Thanks pastor," he replied and sat down next to Cindy.

Pastor Warren pulled over one of the metal folding chairs stacked in a corner and sat down across from Bernie and Cindy. In some counseling sessions he preferred to sit close by the counselees rather than sit behind his desk in an effort to promote camaraderie and friendship. He also believed in being touchy-feely. "So how are you doing?" he said as he tapped him on his knee.

"Bernie grinned. "I'm doing fine, thanks," he said then glanced at Cindy and raised his eyebrows.

"That's good news," Pastor Warren replied with a nod. "Now let me give you some real good news," he began emphatically. "The purpose in our pre-marital counseling is to evaluate our candidates' relationship with Christ so we can counsel them based on the Bible's teaching and plan the ceremony accordingly. If they are not Christians then we must go in a different direction. Historically we believe a Bible-based marriage endures over time so we take the opportunity to explain that when you both have a personal relationship with Christ—you receive special blessings that otherwise you would forfeit." He stopped, looked clearly at Bernie and said, "Where do you stand with Jesus?" He asked Bernie first since he believed that the man is to be the spiritual head of the household so it was imperative for him to establish this before going further.

Bernie looked at him in bewilderment then rolled his eyes. "I believe in God and Jesus," he replied then shot a look at Cindy who simply shrugged her shoulders.

Pastor Warren smiled and tapped Bernie's knee once again. "Aahhh! Now that's good!" he affirmed. *A Bible verse out of James flew into his mind: You believe that there is one God. You do well. Even the demons believe—and tremble.* "Now let's go a step further," he said then stared at the both of them. "We're good?"

Bernie bit his lower lip and clutched Cindy's hand as if preparing himself for tougher questions. "Um, I guess so," he replied nervously.

"Okay, so let me explain a fundamental doctrine that we believe here at Meadowbrook church. It's called *regeneration* or being *born-again* and it is a God-given gift that results in salvation. When a person recognizes and confesses that they are a sinner and in need of a Savior—namely Jesus Christ—and they receive him as their own personal Savior, the Holy Spirit regenerates their soul and they are granted the gift of eternal life with Jesus in heaven. So when they die as a believer—they are immediately transported to heaven. Now that's real good news!" He stopped explaining and waited for a response.

Silence.

Frustration.

Bernie grew pensive then gave him a dismissive wave of his hand. "What if I don't believe that stuff? Isn't believing in Jesus enough?" His voice was growly, like he needed to clear his throat. Then he pointed to Cindy. "As long as we love each other, and I might add that our careers have afforded us well which is a sign from God that he is blessing us—why go through all these ramifications? It's too complicated!" Seconds later he looked at Cindy and shook his head. *Let's get out of here!* he thought.

An anonymous thought flashed into Pastor Warren's mind. *Liquor leaves you breathless; drugs leave you senseless; things leave you penniless. Jesus won't leave you regardless.* But he decided not to use it now. He decided to change his tactic. He remembered the conversation he had with his wife over unequally matched marriages and that he was conflicted about marrying non-believers or unmatched couples where one was a Christian, the other was not. But then realized it was God's business to bring people to Christ so his position was that he would present the Gospel at the counseling sessions and the wedding ceremony and let the Holy Spirit work things out.

In the next moment Pastor Warren bent in closer to Cindy. "Now what about you? Where do you stand in all of this? After hearing my explanation of regeneration, what is your relationship with Jesus? I remember what you first told me about your going to church when you were a child, but after hearing me explain regeneration to Bernie—where do you think you stand with God?"

Her eyes flicked to Bernie's face, then away. She looked sad because she knew him intimately and could read his mind. "Now I'm not sure where I am in all of this. If Bernie's upset—?" she paused, "—then maybe we should wait until we sort things out.

"And as far as my relationship with Jesus goes—" she hesitated mid-sentence then added, "—like they say, 'I have to think about it.'"

Pastor Warren waited momentarily before responding to the dismissal response. He would not press the issue of salvation at this point. He remembered Hudson Taylor's remark when it came to salvation: *If your father and mother, your sister and brother, yes, even the very cat and dog in your house are not happier for your being a Christian, it is a question whether you really are one or not.*

Surprisingly, Bernie raised his hand amidst the challenging conversation. "Hold on," he said as tears welled up in his eyes. "I don't want to risk losing Cindy over this whole thing, but I want to please her so can we just get married here without the whole—" he searched for the proper words, "—rigmarole or hassle of our relationship over—what's that word, 'regeneration'?"

Pastor Warren realized that he was only an instrument that God uses when he thought on the text, '. . . *and we know that all things work together for good to those who love God, to those who are called according to his purpose . . .* 'He gave them a thumb up and said, "See my Jenny and set things up with her for your wedding.

Everyone smiled at each other.

* * *

MEADOWBROOK CHRISTIAN CHURCH

Both Bernie and Cindy were delighted to see so many of their family, friends, and coworkers turn out for their unique wedding ceremony and the reception to follow. More than one-third of the church sanctuary was filled with well-wishers and to a degree, seekers, who were curious to see how the marriage ceremony would be conducted at a Christian church when a couple co-habited for years.

For Cindy, having her best friend, Carolyn, as her maid-of-honor, and for Bernie having his co-worker, Marty, as his best man, their day would be very special. *I just knew God would bless this day,* she realized as she scanned the sanctuary while her heart did a fillip. *It's nice to see our parents taking part in this celebration,* she thought as she waved to them sitting in the front pew.

For Pastor Warren and his deacons they also were delighted for the opportunity to present the gospel to so many visitors.

Bernie and Cindy stood in the foyer to the altar waiting for Pastor Warren to call them forward. Bernie in his black suit and Cindy in a white dress held hands and smiled at each other in wonder as if the day was not really happening. *As if it were a miracle.* "Your hands are ice cold!" Cindy chided him.

Bernie gave a long, theatrical sigh followed by a nervous titter. "That's because I'm not use to being in a church and having so many of your family around."

"Better get used to my family, pal," Cindy replied, "we're going to see a lot more of them in the future." *And probably more of church,* she didn't say.

He turned and kissed her on her cheek and teased, "I know—I'm getting the whole package!"

"I'm worth it," she replied just as Pastor Warren signaled them to come forward to stand next to him on the altar. Seconds later he called her dad up along with Cindy's maid of honor and Bernie's best man to join them. Once they were all on the altar the church soloist sang Cindy's favorite song, *Love Changes Everything*.

Pastor Warren deliberately hesitated several moments after the song before speaking to change the mood from celebration to spirituality and solemnity. To him, marriage between a man and a woman was a sacred matter. "Family, church members, guests and seekers, today we are gathered together . . . " he paused his introduction, " . . . that sounded like the traditional ceremony, 'gathered together,' but this occasion is not traditional," he explained, "because I am persuaded that God is going to do something spectacular today.

"When we think of marriage we need to remember that the Bible explains to us that a marriage took place between God and Israel. Israel was considered to be the husband in the relationship. Later in the church age, the church was likened unto the bride of Christ. So we see that marriage plays an important role in God's view and in society—and I might interject here—that Satan knows this and works unceasingly to disrupt that sacred union; both in the church and in the family."

A momentary thought flew into his mind. He remembered that years ago when he was marrying his wife, Sandy, that the pastor added a note of humor into the ceremony. He had pointed to Sandy's left hand and said, "In marriage there are three rings. The engagement ring she already has, the wedding ring she gets today, and the suffer-ring she will have forever." The congregation laughed. But Warren avoided any hint of humor today.

"When a marriage starts out with Christ being the central binding agent in the relationship, the marriage is made to endure—despite hardships that invariably come to every life and marriage," Pastor Warren explained as he tapped his Bible. "Yes, you may think that there are plenty of marriages that have endured over the years where Christ was not central to their relationship. So yes, there are exceptions, but in my view, these marriages unwittingly followed Biblical mandates, unintentionally raised their family under the blessings the Bible affords to those who live lives that follow the Ten Commandments, and innocently follow the New Testament's rules for holy living. That is a recipe for success. There's only one problem with that scenario—" he paused and exhaled deeply. "—where will they spend eternity? The solution is receiving Christ as our personal savior who died on the cross for our sins. It's almost as if Jesus Christ looked down from the cross and said, 'For you I'm doing this.'

"The Bible states, 'Today is the day of salvation,' Pastor Warren explained dramatically. "That means you cannot afford to postpone a decision for Jesus one more day—simply because you could be killed in a car accident on the way home from this wedding ceremony—and not having decided for Christ, wind up in hell for all eternity. No it's too much of a risk to take! Think about this right now—" he paused and signaled his deacons to pray for God to honor his invitation and that there would be a good response. Seconds later he turned to Cindy's dad and motioned for him to escort her into Bernie's arms that symbolized the union of Christ and his church. Then he turned to Bernie and Cindy and said gleefully, "Now let us proceed with the exchanging of vows and rings."

Moments later, Pastor Warren turned to the couple and then toward the church body and announced, "I now pronounce you man and wife. You may now kiss the bride."

Bernie embraced her then just as he was about to kiss her he said just above a whisper, "I do want to be with Jesus and you for all eternity like Pastor Warren explained."

Cindy knew what he meant and replied as tears began to fall, "And so do I!"

"Aahhh! Praise the Lord!" Pastor Warren exclaimed, recognizing their solemn commitment to each other and to the Lord. "Now, as we conclude our ceremony I would like a show of hands to anyone who made a decision for Christ today."

Bernie's best man, Marty along with two visitors to the church raised their hands.

For Pastor Warren, it was a day of miracles.

FUTURE PROPHETIC
EVENTS

THE OPENING OF THE ABYSS

W hen I awakened this morning, my body was shaking uncontrollably. I was panting and perspiring as if I'd been running frantically away from something. My eyes were glassy and my mouth hung in horror as I groped for anything to latch onto; a substance that was real. I grasped hold of the hospital bed and heard myself shout out, "NO! YOU FIENDS MUST GO BACK!" The echo of my cry bouncing off the walls then seemed to bring me around to a feeble consciousness.

"Mr. Cohen, you must rest! Please lie back and try to sleep," the voice pleaded as I fell back into a state of suspended reality. My mind heard the nurse talking to the doctor about me, snickering in disbelief, but I was unable to speak up in my own defense. I knew the horror I had experienced was real, despite what anybody might think. To say that I had a terrible nightmare about some ghoulish invasion would be ludicrous when the event I witnessed truly happened.

But now, as I look out my hospital window here in the ancient city of Jerusalem, seeing the patriarchal memorials and the time-etched hills of Judea, I reasoned that my senses must have been playing games on me. I looked across the room to the mirror on the wall and called upon every ounce of strength to walk over to it. Despite the cast on my ankle, I limped as fast as I could. As I examined myself, I was shocked to see bruises and welts on my body, even wounds on my hands like I'd been crawling over rocks. The open cuts on my face looked as if I were dragged on the ground.

I peered into the mirror with glazed eyes and murmured, "How did this happen? Was I attacked while exploring the caves near Qumran? Had I fallen into a ravine on the outskirts of the Dead Sea?" I reasoned that I must forcibly attempt to free my mind of whatever was gripping it. I needed to concentrate, to write things down as I remember them, this way the mental blockage will yield to some form of sane mindedness.

Lying here in bed and probing my memory, the floating fragments of some bizarre happenings are beginning to take shape. I recall the bus ride to the Wadi Qumran, nearly one hour's drive from Jerusalem, located at the northern end of the Dead Sea. Enroute, I pored over my guide and history books of the region. Curious archeologists had unearthed numerous cryptic volumes written in Assyrian cuneiform by people long since conquered and removed. Interpretations of the text raised many suspicions about a lost people living in and among the desolate mountains encircling the Sea area. The ancient scribes claimed that the caverns in the mountains were actually "tunnels" that formed an elaborate subterranean labyrinth connecting antechambers in the earth's interior. The writings also told of primordial explorations by heroic men from a nomadic tribe who journeyed deep into the caverns, at first to escape Greek and Roman legions during the pogroms, but later to satisfy age-old curiosities about the belly of the earth.

Distortions in folklore over eons of time often result in bizarre stories, obviously grossly exaggerated beyond any degree of truth. Rarely can you find evidence, apart from narrations, to validate claims of the existence of such nomadic people, unless they left artifacts.

But these writings were unique, they contained drawings.

As I looked at the ancient drawings while riding the bus, originally etched on a cavern wall, now reproduced in folklore books, I was drawn to one entitled, "Abaddon, the Keeper of the Pit." The fading image in the text appeared somewhat concealed by the eroding hand of time. The fascinating drawing depicted an angelic-type creature with six wings. Two covered its feet, two loomed over its head in a menacing fashion; while the other two interlaced around his face, allowing only its eyes to pierce through. The cold and unfeeling eyes were no doubt masculine in gender, and they were staring through the wings as if they could invade one's soul. I closed the books and turned to preparing my photography equipment for the tour.

The photography reports to be spectacular in the evening light and I needed images of the famous K-4 cave where the prophet Isaiah's scrolls were found. Hopefully, I mused, I might get a chance to see some "uncharted" caverns as well. But I knew that I would have to leave the group to capture the right moment when the sunlight hit the caves and adjoining landscape. This would be a time when I would need to be alone. Now when I think back, I know that logic was a big mistake.

The tour group became entranced by the guide who explained the history, folklore, and perils of the region. He reminded us of the precarious cliffs and the deep ravines that circled us and that we should not stray from the dedicated observation areas. He also warned us to be alert for uncharted fissures created by the recent earthquake activity in the area. But as I looked into the distance, beyond the K-4 cave, I saw what looked like a magical glow reflecting off the rock surfaces. At once I knew that this needed capturing on film, at any cost, even a scolding from the tour guide.

I slipped away unnoticed and within seconds I was on my own, journeying upwards toward the region of the caves. When I reached the second plateau, I looked back at the touring party, now resembling tiny ants scurrying around, and realized how desolate this area is. *This is a land of rock.* The view is of escarpments, precipices, gorges, huge ravines and then a body of water known as the Salt or Dead Sea. The Sea is thirteen-hundred feet below sea level, one of the lowest points on the earth. This body of water is fed by the Jordan River and has no outlet, and therefore the evaporation by sunlight leaves a great pool of mineral deposits, too salty for any marine life. The realization that there is no other kind of animal life here suddenly came upon me when I scanned the sky to see if any birds were flying. There were none. It is like the region is under a divine curse with only insects inhabiting the land. It was then that I remembered that indeed, this land was cursed by God thousands of years ago. It was here, at the plains of the Dead Sea where the wicked cities of Sodom and Gomorrah were situated. It was here, right in front of me where the Angel of the Lord called down fire and brimstone from heaven to consume the depraved people and their city. Were the ruins of Sodom and Gomorrah under the Dead Sea, entombed by the hand of God, ever to be seen again? I pondered these things as I neared the top of the ridges overlooking the forsaken valley.

Visibility was good. I could see clearly across the canyon while I set up my tripod to photograph the landscape while the sun began to set. I waited for the golden light to spread its rays over the plain, up the mountain and onto the caves to achieve the desired effect. There was little time before the tour group would complete their lectures, so I hurried. Photo composition came easy and within minutes I had preserved on digital drive at least thirty-six quality images that I knew I could sell to an agency back home.

Then without warning, I heard inhuman squealing sounds coming from what appeared to be a newly formed tunnel entrance to a huge cavern just ahead of where I stood. *The earth had opened from the recent earthquake,* I thought. The strident whine was so loud I jumped and knocked over the tripod holding my camera. At once my mind flashed back to the history books, the claims of underground tunnels and the long-lost journeys into unknown depths of the earth. Half-crazed, I believed this to be a divine opportunity to investigate the phenomena; so to satisfy my yearning for adventure, I pressed on.

If only I hadn't.

I lugged the equipment up the mountainside, then cautiously walked into the tunnel leading to a cavern and realized that something supernatural was happening. I needed to be the first to witness it and record the evidence as a digital file as evidence. As my mind raced, I heard loud whistling coming from the visitor's center, far down on the valley floor. *The group was looking and waiting for me*, I thought. I yelled out, "Wait for me! Wait for me!" But in my heart I knew they couldn't hear me. In a frenzy I abandoned my quest for adventure, grabbed my camera gear and started down the side of the mountain. That was when I lost my footing and fell into a shallow ditch, breaking my ankle.

When I revived my eyes opened into utter darkness. I felt my face and realized my vision was blurred by the fall, but I wasn't blinded. This nighttime blackness had engulfed the entire region of the Dead Sea while I lay unconscious. Fear began to grip my soul when I realized that a search party needed launching in daylight. I felt stranded. With the treacherous chasms and unmapped regions brought on by the earthquakes, no one would dare attempt a rescue after dark, so I crawled out of the ditch into the tunnel.

Warm air radiated off the rocks and circulated into the cavern while I lay on the ground. *Small consolation*, I thought, *I won't have to worry about freezing to death in here.* But my fear was not of temperature, but of the silent darkness. A cloak of blackness hung over the entrance of the cavern, forbidding me from seeing out and in turn raising my awareness that there is no sound of life anywhere. Then the thoughts of the squealing returned. Where had they come from? Suddenly I remembered I had a flash unit in my pocket! I switched it on and desperately fired it off at the tunnel walls. The low-powered photoflash only illuminated about twenty-five feet ahead of me, and that was only for a split-second of time. *At least it was some form of security to separate me from the night,* I thought.

As I triggered the flash several times against the walls I saw yellowish smoke emerging from the depths of the cavern, drifting upwards, reaching for freedom outside. I couldn't risk draining the batteries, so I decided to use the flash only in an emergency. It was then that I realized how frightening the intense darkness is.

Within minutes my resolve hardened and I became determined not to allow fear to control me. I recalled being out near the River in Nam when we were on patrol in the Marine Corp. It was right after my partner took a round in the neck. He lasted only long enough to tell me to 'get even' with *Charlie*. But *Charlie* reigned in the bush near the River, and darkness was upon me. So I decided not to try to walk out, but to sit tight until dawn. That was the longest night of my life. I cowered under a fan palm, tucked away in a small pocket of the jungle, listening to the insects. I dare not open any light since *Charlie* was all around me. Sitting motionless, I stared out into the darkness until first light . . .

My mind was beginning to return to the present when suddenly the ground shook under me. Tremors gave way to spasms and within minutes the earth began to unleash the fury of another earthquake. Massive rumblings echoed off the tunnel walls, spiraling downwards through the cavern. Then I heard rock strata shifting beneath me as if preparing an exit from the very bowels of the earth. An eerie dragging started and ended that sounded like a gigantic stone door opening. Then suddenly gusts of smoke pushed out, swirling about, and engulfing me until it located the mouth of the tunnel, then ascended skyward. Light slowly emerged from the cavern that cast a red hue against the walls allowing me to get a glimpse of the tunnel ceiling. Stone archways strengthened the tunnel from collapse, but that was no comfort to me in this blasphemous place. I knew the weird subterranean noises were the beginning of a supernatural unveiling of a hidden horror about to come upon the human race.

I flashed my camera strobe several times toward the underground chamber to light my path as I began to crawl toward the sounds emerging from below. Despite my fear of the unknown, I had to see beyond the rim that lie before me. My eyes became transfixed on the bellowing smoke and the strange objects that were flying out of the pit. The soil under me was trembling in pain and torment from what it was about to unharness.

Why am I curiously being drawn to this unholy event? Had I gone mad? No, I reasoned, *few witness an actual seismic disturbance while inside the earth, especially with a camera in hand. The photographs would be worth the danger, the pain, the fear.* With this resolve, I dragged myself higher, toward the peril before me. Near the ridge, to my horror, I saw drawings on an adjacent wall. I rubbed my eyes, thinking my perception was distorted. Then I squeezed them shut, thinking my mind is playing games; but they were not. The meandering smoke obstructed my view, but I know now that what I saw was real. Despite the smoke and intense heat, determination forced me to see the images more clearly.

While dragging my limp leg behind me, I reached the opening of the crevasse. Once atop the ridge, overlooking the great fissure, the drawings came into full view. The giant chasm reminded me of a fixed gulf between heaven and hell. The drawings were on the distant wall. I rested, then studied the mosaic-type picture ahead of me. It was like something I had never seen before. It reminded me of a prehistoric mural, telling a story, etched on cave walls by stone-age men. Yet, it was not primitive, but complicated, obviously well thought out and planned—someone making sure that it would be considered genuine.

My first survey of the lifesize drawings revealed a large collage, intricate and cryptic in nature, which resembled a deranged view of Dante's Inferno. One central figure dominated the scene, with subordinate figures surrounding it. The more I looked at it, the more I saw. After several minutes of starring at the images, I saw it—the figure of Abaddon! His shape, camouflaged by the pattern of the drawings, remained concealed unless one closely examined it. While flashing my camera strobe, my eyes pored over the picture to study it, to understand its message. That is when fear overcame me again. The figure of Abaddon was different from the drawings in the book. His body and wings were in the same position, but his feet were visibly crushing the heads of men as they grimaced in anguish. The eyes of his victims told of utter despair. Looking at his eyes, I realized they were almost omnipresent; they were reaching down into my soul. My body squirmed in response. Every fiber of my being recognized the presence of danger.

Perhaps it was fatigue, or even delusion that would explain what happened next. Maybe it really did happen, I'm not sure; but long shadows suddenly were cast on the drawings, shadows that moved. Then I saw the shadows changing form, but my mind would not accept it. Transforming before my eyes, the shadows turned to men-like figures; more like creatures, climbing out of the crevasse. I immediately ceased any movement while observing this incredible occurrence. They were naked, possessing the amazing ability to scale the steep sides of the huge abyss and within seconds were standing on the side of the giant earthen crack, beckoning to something or someone below. I held my breath and dared not move. They were no more than twenty feet in front of me, but the darkness shielded me. They looked out toward the exit, then at each other, and seemed to communicate a form of strategy. I pulled myself together just in time to stifle a scream as I studied their features. These grotesque beings were unlike anything I had ever seen. Their towering height had to be at least seven feet, while their frames were gaunt and emaciated as if they had never eaten, nor ever would. Tightly stretched skin revealed their skeletons, and although I knew little about anatomy, I recognized the absence of many vital bones that make up humans. Having no rib cages or pelvic bones simplified the necessary structure to enable them to maneuver about. It seemed they lacked organs and therefore did not need protective bones.

As they looked around methodically, I gulped in horror as I saw only three narrow horizontal slits where a face should be. They had no mouth or ears. They could not have been of this earth.

The dust from the bellowing pit reached my nostrils and I felt myself begin to sneeze. "Oh no," I whispered. I thought they heard me so I froze with fear as the creatures glanced around, then darted off down the tunnel out into the darkness of the Dead Sea region. A surge of relief came over me as I pushed myself toward the edge of the huge fissure. I reached the place where the creatures had been standing, then looked in terror at their footprints embedded in the dirt. They resembled two pairs of saw-toothed nippers fanning out in different directions from a central pad on the foot. *What kind of demonic entity could this be?*

An insane curiosity overpowered me; I had to see into this cleavage in the earth. I slithered on my belly to the very precipice of the pit, exercising every bit of strength I had, and as I did, the wailing sound intensified. Suddenly I sniffed in disgust at a foul odor permeating the cavern air all around me. When I looked over the ragged edge of the chasm, I saw that it had no bottom! All that I could see was vast emptiness.

My senses however, detected a presence below of a busy network leading to some unknown region. *Perhaps rooms flanking a huge chamber where the horrible groanings were coming from?* I reasoned. I quickly realized that what my eyes couldn't see in the blackness, my ears heard. There not only was a wail, but moans and howls besides—even screams—which no mortal could ever utter. This dreadful dirge had not just started up either, it sounded as if they had dwelled down there since time began. These sounds had to be coming from alien denizens who inhabit the very corridor leading to hell.

I reached over the precipice of the chasm to catch whatever kept flying out, but the searing hot air from the inferno below nearly burned my flesh, so I quickly withdrew my arm. When I did, earsplitting squealing started up. I then realized these winged things were communicating with something back down in the nether world from which they came. I gazed into the expanse and perceived that something like insects kept whizzing by me, seeking the air above the wretched pit. So I thrust my hand into the air current and grabbed one of them. I gave it a quick glance and saw in the dim light radiating off the cavern walls, what looked like a deformed locust with a tiny face of a man! I gasped in disbelief, then slammed it against the ground and threw my handkerchief over it. The squeals then changed to a deafening buzz as if their defenses were penetrated. The call intensified until a massive swarming took shape. Right there I cringed and prayed to the Lord for deliverance from this macabre expulsion of nature.

Scanning the area, I saw at least a hundred thousand or more of these diabolical locusts hovering over the newly formed gorge. They lingered above me as if they were getting instructions. Exhausted and scared beyond human endurance, I began to retreat from the ledge of the chasm. But as I did, I heard a distinct human rattling, perhaps metallic voices, coming from that lower place. Enthralled, and acting like a fool, I pushed myself back up.

By now there were many swarms up and down the rift; millions of locusts—buzzing in cadence as if listening to a voice emanating from that damned cavity that would direct their mission. *Gehenna*, I thought, *this must be the very passageway to the abode of the doomed.* I had to see more, so I inched back up to the side of the gulf to listen again. "I am your king, Abaddon," the rumbling, rasping voice said as it rebounded off the walls of the escarpment. "Go out and afflict pain and suffering on men, biting them like scorpions." Then the whine of the swarms peaked to a shriek as they darted up and out the tunnel. I had hoped the nightmare was over, but it was not.

After the hordes of locusts took off, I heard coming from a different, deeper compartment, a series of guttural yowls. I shook my head and murmured, "All sorts of deviate spirits must be dwelling down there." Then I heard heavy chains dragging against massive stones.

These shackled fiends then bellowed out, "FREE US FROM HERE!"

Without warning the ground began vibrating and shaking under me. *Another quake?* I asked myself. I muffled my mouth and whispered, "It will suck me in! Oh no!" But this was not a quake, but the closing of the abyss, the trachea—the evil sphincter—the very entrance that led to the bottom of the earth's breathing apparatus—the damned pit of hell. Slowly and resolutely the jaws of the chasm closed until the lightless crevasse was sealed shut.

Abruptly afterwards, a whoosh of air encircled me. I sensed something unseen moving right next to me. Invisible, yes, but I could feel it's awful presence. I turned cold and numb, like a dead man. I squeezed my eyes shut and waited. Time seemed to stop. After a while, I opened my eyes, only to see those ghastly paw prints again; this time in front of me, leading out of the chasm, up into the tunnel. I shuddered and went limp.

Terror-stricken, I lie motionless in front of the crevasse. I needed to regain my strength. I raised my head and looked down the pit in utter resignation. What did all this mean? Could this be a signal of the end of the world? If so, how could I ever warn the world before it was too late? Who would believe it? With that, a surge of fatigue overwhelmed me as I rolled over, staring at the ceiling of the cavern watching the last remnants of smoke ascend out the tunnel, drifting out into space . . .

The chronicle is now complete. I was rescued early in the morning by the authorities and airlifted to the hospital in Tel Aviv where I now lie in my bed. But as I recount this ghoulish experience, I can't keep the name, 'Abaddon' out of my head. The name is haunting me. Where did I hear that name before yesterday? Did I read it? In anguish, I pounded my bedside then massaged my temples to jog my memory. Where is that name? Where?

I then shuffled across the room to the cabinet by the washbasin, and took out my cell phone and entered in the Google search the word 'Abaddon.' When the title came up my fingers were shaking as I read in the dictionary section, 'Abaddon: the fallen angel appointed as the custodian over the demons in Tartaros; the abode of the evil spirits who had sexual relations with mortal women before the Noahic Flood. These condemned angels will be released on the world before the Second Coming of Christ. [See Revelation Chapter Nine and Jude verse Six.]'

"GOD HELP US!" I cried aloud as I staggered back to my bed.

After fumbling through Google again, I managed to locate the other passage: 'And the angel received the key to the bottomless pit . . . and there came out of the smoke, locusts, who are told to hurt the unbelievers. They had the face of a man with hair like a woman. Their teeth were like a lion . . . and they had a king over them whose name in the Hebrew tongue is *Abaddon* . . . and the four other angels were let loose . . . ' I shook my head in despair, then slumped onto my bed. "This can't be," I muttered. Then I threw my head back in awesome relief while realizing I'm protected from harm because I am a believer on Christ. Reading again I went to the reference at Jude verse six: ' . . . and the fallen angels were cast out of heaven and reserved in everlasting chains in darkness until the judgment of the last day.' "What will it be like now that they're loose?" I whispered to myself as I gazed out the window. *No doubt the four creatures I saw were those fallen angels*, I summarized, as a wave of resignation came over me. *What is the use, I cannot alert anybody, no one would believe this fantastic story without some tangible proof*, I reasoned. Then I remembered something. I hobbled as quickly as I could to the clothing closet and rummaged through my pants. I reached into my pocket and then a great relief overpowered me as I pulled out my dirty handkerchief containing the mangled dead locust . . .

THE CORRIDOR TO HEAVEN

C hrissy gazed into the mirror hanging on her bedroom wall, saw her reflection, then burst into tears. She couldn't believe how terrible she looked. Peering at the glass, she then pinched her cheek and cried out, "What is happening?"

Only her echo resounding off the walls answered.

Why was I left behind? she thought. *Has it been only a few days?* Realizing her solitude once again, panic struck. She ran into her brother's room, then to her parents room, hoping they had returned, but in her heart she knew they never would. Writhing in anguish she staggered to the kitchen, then crumpled to the floor sobbing. Exhaustion quickly brought on a wave of sleep.

Her world was altogether different now; being radically altered by the determined hand of God. She was no longer an aspiring college junior seeking a degree in Political Science from a Long Island University, nor the pretty daughter of an electronic engineer. No, she was now a desperate sort of survivor looking for answers behind the global disappearance that claimed her family and innumerable others.

Summoned to consciousness by the incessant beeping of her cell phone, Chrissy fumbled her way to the phone and hit the TALK button. "Chrissy, is that you?" the voice asked.

"Cindy!" Chrissy screamed at the phone.

"Thank God! I've been calling you for so long. . .I thought maybe you too were taken," Cindy added in relief. There was a momentary pause, then Cindy asked as she viewed the image on her phone, "Are you alright? You look—"

"I know, I haven't slept in a few days, since. . ." she said lamely as she looked around the room. She felt her face then stepped closer to the phone, ". . .since everyone just vanished." Casting her eyes away from the screen, she sighed and added, "I was afraid to leave the house. After that blaring sound from the sky and when it turned fiery red, I just wanted to go and hide. Then I heard over the TV what happened, you know. . ." she groped for more words, ". . .the President's announcement. Then there were all the news clips of the related calamities, the mass hysteria, the looting and the suicides, I really got scared."

"Your parents? Your brother?" Cindy inquired.

"All gone. I'm all alone now. . ." she trailed off before going mute.

"Chrissy!" Cindy ordered. "Snap out of it!"

Numbed and confused, Chrissy sought to silence her phone.

"Wait! Just hang on. I'm coming over. I'll stay with you!" Cindy said. "I'll be there in fifteen minutes, just don't lose hope or panic." Then the phone went silent. Chrissy then turned to look out the window and watch for her friend.

She scanned the neighbor's houses and stopped at Gail's, her mother's best friend. Then a new wave of despair swept over her as she recalled how upset she became when Gail's little boy, Raymond, deflated the tires on their new car one morning while they slept. She muffled a smile when she remembered the devilish gleam in his eyes when she caught him fleeing from the scene. But new or old cars didn't matter now, and somehow smiles just didn't seem to fit any more as she looked at their uninhabited home. *Where did everybody go?* In her heart she really knew. Fear once again gripped her senses as the realization arrived that this was not a nightmare, but stark reality.

Turning toward the kitchen table while stifling her tears, she groaned when she saw the table still set for the family dinner of three days ago. On the chairs lay another startling reminder of her family's hasty departure. The very clothes they were wearing that day hung in disarray as if the bodies were suddenly yanked upwards, leaving the garments behind. She shook her head in disbelief as she began to fill up with tears once again.

Without warning there was a loud crash outside her house.

She ran to the door and saw Rusty, the gas station attendant, holding his bleeding head as he ran toward her. His car collided with one of the abandoned cars left in the street. "My God, Chrissy, what is happening to us?" he yelled before he collapsed on her lawn. She quickly grabbed a moist towel from the kitchen, ran to his side, and wiped his brow until he revived.

"Rusty, are you okay?" she asked as he shook his head as if to regain his senses.

He looked around, remembered where he was, felt his head, and replied, "Just smacked my head on the dashboard, I wasn't concentrating on where I was going. I can't believe what is going on—my mother and father—they disappeared—then there were these creatures. . ." he trailed off in a daze.

Chrissy glared at him, then smacked him in the face until he was alert once again. She walked him over to the porch where they sat down on the steps. "What creatures?" Chrissy asked, hoping he was hallucinating.

His hands motioned in the air and his face grimaced as if he were reliving the incident. "I was at work and raced home after everyone disappeared, only to find my mother and father's clothes just piled on the living room floor, the TV still on—I searched the house—but found nothing. I sat crumpled on the floor next to their clothes wondering what to do. I must have been there for hours." He looked into Chrissy's eyes in desperation and asked, "What should I do now?"

Chrissy patted him softly to console him and asked again, "Rusty, what creatures?"

"THEY'RE FIENDS! THEY'RE DEMONS FROM THE PIT OF HELL!" he screamed at her as he suddenly remembered the nightmare. He leaped from the steps, pointed his finger at her and said with a shaking voice, "They came out of the earth! I saw the ground open right after the disappearance, and they just climbed out as if being released from some kind of subterranean prison. They were ghastly looking, like some kind of ghouls from the grave. There were so many I couldn't count them. They streamed out and ran off in all directions." He bolted towards his car and shouted, "Get out of here before they get you!" Within seconds he was in his car, looked around frantically, and turned on the ignition. The front end was damaged, but the engine roared into life as he floored the gas pedal and sped away.

Chrissy cowered in the kitchen corner. Her eyes surveyed the room and stopped on the wall calendar for 2026. In large bold print she read: 'Havenville Pharmacy.' *Some haven*, she thought. A *'haven' is supposed to be a place of safety, a place of shelter.* She bobbed her head in contempt and murmured, "There will never be a safe place in Havenville ever again."

* * *

On the drive over, Cindy filled her ears with radio broadcasts. It was all too incredible to believe. Nuclear war looked like it could break out at any point. Russian-backed, Syrian-Iranian forces along with China were poised to attack and penetrate Israel through occupied Lebanon. At first, the United States refused Israel support due to public disfavor, but later relented and decided to honor their treaty. American President Randolph sent thirty divisions of Marines to safeguard her borders along with two nuclear-powered aircraft carriers to stand on station in the waters off Haifa. Unofficial reports told of the breakdown of negotiations between the UN, Tehran, and Damascus.

The newscast then localized the global crisis by adding that Floridians were especially frightened. Before the war scare, local civil defense officials published studies revealing Florida's unpreparedness for war. With nuclear research labs and nuclear power plants, along with several military bases, the peninsula was a prime target. Inadequate evacuation routes which make escape nearly impossible didn't help matters either. Then as an added problem, there were entirely too few fallout shelters to handle the population. This glum report only heightened the tension in Cindy's mind.

All the roads enroute to Chrissy's house showed signs of the great departure. Innumerable cars with their drivers suddenly snatched, still stood in the center of the roadway, causing her to strategically weave her car to avoid collision. Shopping malls strangely vacant. Public transportation at a standstill. Instead of the usual looting and burglarizing during a crisis, there was an eerie quietness, with people peering out of their windows in their homes—as if they were too scared to go outdoors. Occasionally she saw a police car go racing by, but it looked like they didn't know where to begin to help.

Nearly half an hour had elapsed since their phone conversation occurred, and finally, Cindy arrived at Chrissy's house. As soon as she heard the car door slam, Chrissy dashed to the front door to meet her girlfriend. "Oh thank God! I'm so glad to see you," Cindy said wildly. They hugged each other until their nerves steadied, then entered the house.

Cindy was always dependable during a crisis. Her self-confidence enabled her to be resourceful and at times independent; sometimes going to the extreme of shutting people out when they disappointed her. Now as Chrissy's best friend, she would have to tap every ounce of strength to meet her needs.

Chrissy's condition, along with the disorder of the confused community began to grate on Cindy's nerves. She became uneasy, as if she knew they were in deep trouble. After settling Chrissy down on the living room sofa, she proceeded to make something to eat. Despite her usual calmness and stamina, Cindy did become frazzled even more after taking sight of Chrissy's family's clothes strewn on the kitchen chairs. She decided to serve the makeshift supper in the dining room.

Chrissy responded nicely to Cindy's care. Once she began to eat, she felt better. "Chrissy, we must talk this out. We're in this together, and we have to face it—we must go on," Cindy said to encourage dialog.

"I saw the whole thing you know. I saw them all go up to—" Chrissy blurted out, then stopped cold. She then caught and transfixed her eyes on the TV in the living room. Puzzled, Cindy looked askance towards the TV, then back to Chrissy.

"The whole thing. Go up?" Cindy echoed.

"You may think I'm crazy, but I had a vision or dream or whatever, while it was happening! I think I must've been singled out to warn others. They all went up to heaven, my family, countless thousands, everybody just disappeared—they're in heaven now . . ." She continued to stare at the TV while relating the events to Cindy, then closed her eyes and waved her arm and added, "I even saw people, disembodied souls if you will, come drifting out of their graves . . . !"

"Oh come on Chrissy! Calm down!" Cindy cut in as Chrissy's chest heaved with anxiety.

Chrissy got up and moved toward the TV, knelt down to pray and cried out, "Lord, help us to see what to do." With that Cindy ran to her and escorted her back to the sofa.

Suddenly a crashing sound, followed by a window slamming came from the basement. Then a gust of air followed by heavy scraping noises was heard. Cindy jumped, gulped, and yelled, "What was that?" as their eyes darted to the basement door.

The sounds faded as if something scurried off, then the basement was quiet again. "Probably a stray cat hit the stick holding up the basement window. Fool thing is likely playing in the empty boxes," Chrissy replied as she appeared to come out of a trance.

"Must have been a Godzilla-sized cat by the sound of it," Cindy said catching her breath and dismissing it.

Chrissy looked at an imaginary spot on the wall and recalled her vision, "I seem to remember now. There was a huge corridor, maybe two miles wide, that extended from the earth right into the red sky, then up into deep space; there were many worldwide.

"Thousands upon thousands simply floated through the air up the corridor in streams," she paused, sighed and added, " . . . then I saw . . . a glimpse of my family going up. They didn't really have bodies like ours, but theirs were beautiful and glowed like the pictures I've seen of Jesus on the Mount of Transfiguration. They were alive and breathing, yet they were no longer mortal, they were like divine beings." As if reminiscing, she turned to look at the family portrait hanging on the wall, then fell back onto the sofa, exhausted.

Cindy was a born skeptic. The story sounded too farfetched for her. Yet she wondered, where did all those people go to? And there were countless other questions left unanswered. "Chrissy, my family and I are still here, but yours are gone, how come? Was it a 'religious thing' like the news media claimed?"

Determined not to relapse into a depressed state, Chrissy sat up brightly and rebounded. "I'm beginning to believe that God took my family and all the others in the 'Rapture.' But, because I scoffed at their faith—refusing to acknowledge Jesus Christ for who He was and that I needed to make a personal application of His death on the cross—I, along with many others, remained behind. To what end? I don't know yet, but I have some ideas." She went to her laptop and began pointedly punching entries into the keyboard. Puzzled, she paused into deep thought and whispered, "If only I could remember those Bible verses, maybe . . ."

Cindy interrupted her thoughts, "What is the 'Rapture' anyway?"

"I remember my Dad speaking about it often. It is s theological term referring to a time when all those 'in Christ' will be taken up to heaven, while they're still alive! They will be changed or 'translated,' as my Dad would say quoting his commentary, from an earthly body to a heavenly one, instantaneously."

"Hmm . . . that's interesting. I never heard about that," Cindy noted.

Chrissy continued, "My family wasn't even afraid of the war. Being Christians, my Dad said, 'that regardless of any war scare, that God would protect them.' He had faith in 'his Savior,' as he put it, and that if a real danger existed, they would be miraculously removed. My mother and brother believed the same way. I was the rebel.

Forgetting: "Now what was I about to key in—"?

Cindy mused momentarily, then queried further, "Weren't you convinced of what they believed?"

"I saw their lives change and their devotion to the Lord, but we wanted different things from life," Chrissy replied. "True, there was no mistaking the joy in their hearts, but I thought 'happiness' was the same as joy. You see, I wanted to push out and make my mark in the world; they were content with their lives. I wanted to run with a fast crowd at school who enjoyed the good times; they preferred Bible studies. I desired 'things'; they avoided them. They maintained that they needed a personal relationship with Christ; I felt the knowledge I had of Him was enough." She threw up her hands and added, "They preached to me every day, but I just wouldn't listen. Now look where I am," she concluded glumly.

Cindy took notice of the telecast and turned the volume up. Horrible scenes of public transportation calamities plaguing the nation passed in review. Train derailments, aircraft, and taxi-cab crashes, all caused by the sudden removal of drivers and pilots were featured. The gruesome statistics numbering the dead then flashed across the screen. Then the cameras were recording the devastating earthquakes throughout the world. The announcer mentioned that these tragedies, along with the mysterious disappearance, brought the world's population down by an estimated fifteen million.

Apart from the national emergency, the commentator noted that the Armed Forces suffered a drastic reduction in personnel in the disappearance, leaving the nation dangerously vulnerable to enemy attack. The bleak update ended with the ominous note that United States surveillance satellites confirmed a massive Russian and Iranian alliance troop build-up along the Lebanese border. The commentator added that the Pentagon viewed the build-up as an acute peril since American military posture had been downsized by previous administrations, and now was crucially endangered because of the disappearance.

Frightened by the reports, Cindy turned away to Chrissy and said, "Tell me more about this business with the 'corridor.'"

Chrissy settled in the sofa again, squeezed her eyes shut briefly to concentrate, then expounded on her vision. "My vision took place in slow motion, while the actual event probably only lasted two seconds. You remember when it happened, don't you? Everybody does. It will be like when our President Kennedy was assassinated—everybody remembers where they were when they found out about it." She scratched her head to help her remember and added, "It was during that bizarre electrical storm.

"I was sick in bed with the flu. I was called downstairs for an early dinner, just as the sky quickly turned overcast with lightless, looming clouds. I meandered over to the window and looked up as it suddenly turned red. I knew that had to be some weird atmospheric testing program, or else some divine intervention into the weather pattern," Chrissy paused and asked, "Where were you?"

"I was in the bank vault when it happened," Cindy replied. "We were closing for the day. On my way to the vault, I glanced out the window and saw the clouds forming up; I thought it was a mere storm at first, then went about my work. After that I didn't see a thing; it was all over when I got out. Of course we all saw the catastrophic aftermath: accidents, crashes; piles of clothes everywhere. . ." she paused and then motioned for Chrissy to continue.

"Rapid-fire lightning bolts flashed within the heavy crimson clouds. The strokes began arcing to the earth and buildings below. Everybody ran for cover. The flashes intensified into a strobe-like pattern, striking trees, cars, even people below. Within seconds thunder boomed so loudly that the walls vibrated, the ceilings cracked, things flew off the shelves and walls, and the echoes seemed to reverberate off every surface. What made it even more scary was that the rainfall never came.

"By this time I was so scared I ran to my bedroom and grabbed the blanket off my bed, covered my head and just hid in the corner, hoping the roof wouldn't come crashing in. I managed to mutter, 'Mom,' but I didn't get an answer. Then a strange lull occurred, a great calm.

"I curiously looked out the window into the freak darkness and saw certain clouds in the distance begin to swirl and form a circular opening. Streams of super-bright light then shot out in rays from the aperture, gracefully spreading out to form a tremendous passageway—!"

"No one else saw this part, you know," Cindy blurted out. "Once the lightning stopped, the people just disappeared."

Chrissy shook her head with conviction and said, "I only know what I saw. No doubt, my revelation details beyond what the world was allowed to see; I'm like some kind of selected prophetess or something. Although there were masses of people standing stiff with fear, looking towards the clouds waiting for something to happen, obviously only the Christians and myself saw the rest." She walked to the large living-room picture window, opened the drapes, and looked at the sky. "Then I heard some crazy trumpet blaring. This blast was so loud and deafening, I had to cup my ears with my hands. With that, beams and rays of light focused on the Havenville Cemetery, going from grave to grave, in a searching fashion—as if selecting certain plots. Then those gravesites began to glow until the soil and the grass on top began to shake and tingle as if the inhabitants were about to be sucked out and then came the shout." Chrissy sighed in an effort to recapture the vivid scene in her mind.

"The shout?" Cindy asked, pressing for more, "you heard a voice?"

"This was no ordinary voice. This was a call from heaven, an announcement. In fact, I still hear the exact words bellowing in my mind, 'come forth!' was the proclamation. Wasn't that what Christ said to Lazarus before raising him from the dead?

"Then I saw the graves and the crypts free their tenants! It was awesome! They first materialized, then took on a radiant look as if imbued with some type of electrical charge, then simply drifted upwards into the corridor. And then—" her eyes began to water as she recounted the scene, "—as I looked up, my mouth hung open in wonder as innumerable angels in the form of beautiful men appeared at the sides of the great corridor to act as celestial escorts. The refulgent rays emitted from heaven soon gave way to a soft bluish irradiation that signaled what must have been 'phase two'—"

A STRANGE NOISE!

Cindy suddenly bolted upright and yelled, "Did you hear that?!" She jumped to her feet and ran to a back window. "I heard something heavy being dragged into the backyard. It sounded like a canvas sack being pulled along on the ground, heading toward your house."

Chrissy pooh-poohed Cindy's clamor away, shook her head and said, "I didn't hear anything. You're getting as bad as me for heaven's sake; you're all tensed up now. *Relax.* We have had problems with stray cats roaming the neighborhood. They're probable having a party in the backyard by now."

Cindy peered out the rear window, sighed in relief, and said, "It sure is black out there. Nightfall seems to have come very early tonight." She looked down at her watch and saw that it was only four o'clock in the afternoon. She scratched her cheek, looked back out the window and added, "This is very unusual that it would get dark so early this time of the year. And this darkness seems to be so different, even supernatural." She strolled back to the sofa and rationalized the phenomenon away. "Just tired I guess, over-reacting. Sorry about the interruption, please continue. You were saying, 'phase two.'"

Chrissy collected her thoughts. "Yes, they, the angels, began waving their arms with beckoning gestures, to all Christians to come forward. They flanked the immense corridor which then took on the appearance of a huge stairway. Then opalescent beams shot out from the shaft way where it met the clouds and radiated out in all directions. The rays then individually sought out living Christians like a tractor beam and began to pull them up. Just then, Dad, Mom and Georgie appeared in the distance. I screamed for them, but they were looking up and didn't hear me.

"At first they began to turn a bright white, giving way to a dazzling flash. Then the horizon glowed from the many emanations until it formed a brilliant multi-colored spectrum that resembled sunlight refracting through diamonds. Suddenly there was a gigantic 'whoosh' of air followed by a blur so big that it obscured my entire view. Then they were gone. My family—the people—all gone!

"A trail of light lingered on the huge shaft way for several seconds until a loud 'thwack' sounded, then the corridor vanished. It was like the slamming of an enormous door in the sky. I yelled out, 'Daddy!' then ran downstairs to the kitchen only to see their clothes draped on the chairs. The next thing I remembered was your call." Chrissy flopped down on the floor, then dropped backwards, exhausted, as if she just relived the event.

Cindy was visible shaken. She began to pace the floor frantically, then began to sob, "What are we going to do? What is going to happen to us?"

Chrissy was rebounding. "We've got to pull together to find the answers. We'll be alright," she consoled. She realized that Cindy couldn't take much more. Her nerves were shot. Strangely enough, she always projected the image of being together when involved in a crisis, but now that she was helpless against God's hand, she was crumbling fast. Chrissy reached for her hand and prayed aloud, "God in heaven, help us. Forgive us for rejecting your Son, Jesus Christ, and His plan of salvation. We ask for your mercy and guidance for our future." She looked up into Cindy's eyes and saw fresh tears. Tears of peace.

As if a sudden revelation occurred, Chrissy blinked her eyes twice and blurted out, "I remember! I remember!" With that she darted over to her laptop.

"Remember what?" Cindy asked.

"The Bible verses. It was in First Corinthians." She switched to the Bible app and keyed in 'Trumpet.' Seconds later the screen came alive:

> Lo! I tell you a mystery. We shall not all sleep, but we shall all be changed, in a moment, in the twinkling of an eye, at the last trumpet. For the trumpet will sound, and the dead will be raised imperishable, and we shall be changed. [I Cor. 15:51-52 RSV].
>
> —See Commentary on 'Rapture.'

They looked at each other, then Chrissy said, "Humph, 'shall be changed . . . in the twinkling of an eye . . . for the trumpet shall sound . . .' very interesting." She then typed in, 'Commentary,' 'Rapture.' The monitor read:

> Resurrection of the Church known as the Rapture. To be followed by an unprecedented seven-year period known as the 'Tribulation' which culminates in the Second Coming of Christ.
>
> —See also: I Thessalonians 4:16-17 RSV.

Chrissy watched the screen intently and said, "I remember the term 'Tribulation' from my Dad." She then keyed in the additional passage.

> For the Lord himself will descend from heaven with a shout of command, with the archangel's call, and with the sound of the trumpet of God. And the dead in Christ will rise first; then we who are alive, who are left, shall be caught up together with them in the clouds to meet the Lord in the air; and so we shall always be with the Lord. [I Thessalonians 4:16-17 RSV]

She turned to Cindy and said, "That's it! That's what happened! This explains my vision, this prophecy is what the media has dubbed, 'the Disappearance.'"

Cindy nodded, then shook her head and asked, "What about the 'Tribulation'?" Chrissy then punched the keyboard hurriedly. Her eyes widened as she read:

> TRIBULATION: In the Bible this is a period of unparalleled suffering which will proceed the Second Advent of Christ. The trouble will embrace the entire earth. Catastrophic judgments and

punishments will be poured out on mankind. Wars, earthquakes, pestilences, incurable diseases and unprecedented demonic activity shall befall the earth. This is also the period that will experience the supernatural rise to power of the Anti-Christ. For detailed information, key in individual topics. [See also: HOLY BIBLE, Daniel Chapter 9; Matthew Chapter 24; Revelation Chapter 9-11].

"UGH!" Chrissy muttered as she hit the OFF switch. Bewildered, they silently exchanged glances.

"Looks like we're in for a tough time," Cindy concluded.

"With God's help we'll make it 'till Jesus comes for us," Chrissy said with renewed resolve, "and I'm sure there must be others out there who now believe as we do. The *Rapture* had to turn a lot of skeptics and agnostics toward God."

"Maybe we could share, starting with my relatives, what God has revealed to us," Cindy volunteered brightly.

Then the door to the basement suddenly flew violently open.

It crashed against the wall with such force that one hinge came loose. Then a dank green and brown mist crept up the stairs and quickly fanned out in all directions on the floor. The mist gave off a foul stench that smelled of death and the nether world.

Cindy screamed and ran to shut the door. "We now know that was no cat we heard—something evil is down there!" With their hearts pounding in their chests, they fiercely pushed the sofa across the floor to block the door. But as they reached the door, a mutated arm reached through the door trying to grab them.

"AH!" Cindy gasped as it nearly seized her. They jumped aside but held the sofa in place as the horror continued to unfold.

"Look!" Chrissy yelled as she pointed to the center of the living room floor. Rising slowly through the floor was a hairless, man-sized creature with taut rubbery skin that had slits for eyes and two small holes for a nose. It had no mouth but gave off muffled squeals like a wounded rat.

It suddenly stood erect on the floor, watching their every move.

"It's an evil spirit, or demon—or SOMETHING!" Chrissy screamed. "It's one of those things Rusty warned us about. We've got to—"She looked around for a weapon, a knife, a hammer, a club, anything, "—we're being invaded by fiends!"

They both ran to the corner of the room, their eyes riveted on the creature before them. The thing raised its arm at them and then emitted a strident wail that almost deafened. "My ears!" Chrissy screeched as she shot a glance towards the kitchen. Sensing their fear, the entity motioned towards them as they gagged in terror. "RUN FOR IT!" Chrissy shrieked.

The creature then lunged for them as they fled to the kitchen, then stopped and aimed its finger at them. Suddenly the kitchen furniture jumped up in the air and crashed against the outside door. "We're trapped!" Cindy exclaimed. Then the damned spirit from the bottomless pit reached into thin air and pulled out a fireball and hurled it at them. It missed them but flames quickly engulfed the room as the inhuman attacker cornered them.

"IN THE NAME OF JESUS I COMMAND YOU TO STOP!" Chrissy cried out with every fiber in her body.

The hellish figure stopped short and trembled. It then let out a garbled howl, then faded away. Chrissy grabbed Cindy's hand and rushed out the front door as the fires consumed the house.

From the yard they saw several shadowy gnome-like creatures escaping out of the basement window. The leader then pointed, signaled the others, then began to close in on them.

"My car!" Cindy yelled out.

Refusing to look back, they drove down the expressway towards Cindy's house. They now knew that their purpose in life was to be a part of the great evangelistic multitude that would come to believe on Christ during the Tribulation.

CAUGHT UP

BAYSHORE, WYOMING

T he assignment for news reporter Maureen Flynn and her videographer Charlie Adams was a strange one. With a graduate degree in journalism, Maureen at age thirty-five was certainly qualified to cover any sudden catastrophes in America. The editor of the Chronicle where they were employed carefully reviewed the reports from all the national and local news outlets but he needed a first-hand account of the disaster. She was told to travel from Bayshore, Wyoming, to Cody, Wyoming, and carefully document what they saw. In the editor's mind there had to be a rational explanation for the sudden disappearance of millions of people from the earth. He needed to determine if the disappearance was local or widespread.

Troubled in spirit on the way to Cody she needed several moments of quietness to settle her anxiety. While Charlie drove and listened to the news on the car radio, Maureen stared out her window at the clouds, seeking some semblance of peace from nature. She remembered as a child when she would lay down on the grass looking at the beautiful array of clouds and thinking how she would love to jump from one to another wondering what it would feel like to lay down on a soft cloud. Then there were similar thoughts of when she would look at the nighttime sky and see thousands of stars sparkling on a cold winter's night. Or she would love to just watch the firefly's dancing in her backyard.

Why am I experiencing this eerie feeling of loss? she thought. *The clouds are still in the sky and the sun is still shinning but the quiet is unnerving*

"You okay?" Charlie asked, shattering her reverie. He noticed she was unusually subdued.

"Just observing and thinking," she replied softly. "We've been driving for miles and all I see is deserted machinery, stranded cars without drivers, miles of plowed fields and dairy farms and silos filled with grain as well—all without workers—only emptiness. It's really scary!"

Charlie turned off the radio then lowered his window and pulled to the side of the road. "What strikes me first is the stillness of everything. I can't help but cry out, what happened?" He turned to her with a smile and whispered in wonder, "Could this be a UFO flap?" He was a zealous devotee of the Roswell Report by the United States Air Force that has found itself in American folklore since the 1940s.

Maureen looked at him in bewilderment. There has been a huge interest of late about UFOs. *Maybe they're right. Has earth been invaded by aliens? Taken captives like in the movie Close Encounters of the Third Kind? There has to be answers* and she was determined to find out. *No, I don't want my imagination to conjure up all sorts of evil scenarios about what could have happened.* "Hopefully we'll find some explanations when we get to Cody since they have probably been alerted by the media about the great disappearance."

* * *

CODY, WYOMING

The Cody Town Center was located near the Navaho Reservation. The center held all the judicial offices that included licenses and permits, along with voting for local and national elections. It was also the location for protest gatherings for radical groups who disagreed with political, religious, and lately, sexual orientation issues.

Today would be different.

Maureen discerned that the crowds were angry, frustrated, and fearful the minute they pulled into the parking lot. "This doesn't look good!" she said while gulping in air with hands raised. "We need answers!"

The crowds, probably numbering two hundred plus immediately saw the station lettering on the van and the satellite antenna on the roof and rushed to meet them. Within seconds the multitude surrounded them shouting, "WHAT IS GOING ON? TELL US NOW!"

"They think we know what happened!" Charlie exclaimed.

As soon as they stepped out of the van Maureen held up her hand in helpless frustration and yelled trenchantly while patting the air, "CALM DOWN AND LET US SPEAK!" Charlie took the opportunity to capture the anger and fear in the crowds by putting his digital video camera on *Record* and nonchalantly scanned the crowd while they were screaming. Then he turned the camera toward the front entrance of the Town Center and saw armed guards blocking the doors.

"We have been assigned to investigate what has happened," Maureen said haltingly.

"We can't get any answers here!" a spokesperson in the crowd shouted at Maureen as he pointed toward the guards blocking the entrances. "Help us! Where did everyone go?"

An aged woman stepped to the front and reported with eyes blazed, "Everyone here has someone missing either from their family or their friends. Some are parents, children, others are sisters or brothers or neighbors. Do you think there have been mass murders? No! Can't be," she reasoned. "There are no bodies anywhere."

Both Maureen and Charlie shrugged their shoulders. "We will find out," Maureen promised.

A teenage girl pushed through the crowd with eyes widening in shock. "Do you—do ya—think UFOs are responsible?" she gabbled. "Will they—will they—bring them back?"

"We wish we had the answers for you," Maureen replied in frustration. "We can only promise that we will not stop searching for the answers you need. As we continue on this journey to discover truth, we will publicly report our findings."

Charlie nudged her and pointed to the arrival of several police cars. "We need to go!"

Many in the crowd shook their heads in frustration as others motioned they would storm the Town Center regardless of the police and force the civil leaders to give them answers. What they didn't realize is that the civil leaders had no answers.

* * *

Back in the van, Charlie suddenly realized something. He turned reflexively to Maureen and said, "I've been so caught up in this disappearance thing I forgot about my mom." Then he pulled out his cell phone and speed-dialed his mother's number. He let it ring ten times. Then he grew pensive before turning to Maureen. "No answer. Very strange."

Maureen shook her head in disgust as a melding of eerie thoughts tumbled in her consciousness. "What is going on?" she mumbled.

"Yeah, good question," Charlie replied as he drove out of the parking lot. Then, as if divine revelation occurred he suddenly pulled over to the side of the road and stopped the van. "I just remembered my mom telling me about some Bible prophecies that spoke about what she called the *Rapture* where Jesus would come back for his believers and they would suddenly disappear and go with him to heaven. Could that be what happened?" His brow furrowed as he glanced at Maureen. "Is it possible—?"

"I never heard about that," Maureen said. "But then, I'm not a churchgoer."

Charlie's eyes suddenly brightened. "I have an idea. Let's go to the closest Christian church to get some answers."

"Maureen nodded in agreement. "Okay, but I'll let you take the lead since—" she paused and wrinkled her nose, "—I haven't been in church since I was in high school."

* * *

LAKEVIEW CHRISTIAN CHURCH

As soon as the approached the Lakeview Christian Church they quickly noticed that the huge parking lot was full of cars. Charlie then stared at Maureen with a serious look. "Uh-oh. Trouble—" His voice was growly like he needed to clear his throat. "Why all the cars on a weekday? There must be a problem," he assumed.

Moments after they stepped out of the van nearly twenty people ran out of the church toward them. "I'm pastor Ron," a middle-aged man wearing jeans and a hoodie said as he stepped out of the crowd who seemed to be very high-strung and agitated. Then he pointed to the van and said forcefully, "You're the media—what is going on—what's happening?"

Charlie set his video camera back in the van and then turned to the pastor. "Can we talk in private?" he asked furtively then shot a look at

Maureen. She was increasingly edgy as Charlie pressed the pastor. She bit her lip then scratched her head several times avoiding his eyes. She was nervous.

"Let's go to my office," Pastor Ron said as he pushed his way through the crowd. Maureen shrugged her shoulders at Charlie and fell in behind them as they rushed to the church entrance.

Pastor Ron's office was located behind the one thousand plus seat sanctuary. Charlie found the office to be gaudy with modern day furniture and several pictures on the wall of Palestinian leaders shaking hands with American presidents. Another picture showed pastor Ron wearing a rainbow shirt with his arm around the national leader of the gay rights movement. When he glanced at his desk he saw two Bibles, one a King James version, the other a Queen James version. Next to the bibles was a framed photograph of pastor Ron and another man around the same age smiling at each other. Slightly confused he scratched his head as both him and Maureen sat down.

"You've been around in your field of breaking news to know—" Pastor Ron began as he nervously kneaded his temples, "—what's happening?"

Charlie wiggled in his chair then in staccato fashion: "Not sure—maybe a UFO flap. Maybe God got rid of the world's religious radicals—the troublemakers—maybe some government experiment gone haywire."

"Tell him about your mother," Maureen interjected. "You know—the *Rapture* thing." Immediately her words generated tension in the room. "Her disappearing—"

Pastor Ron waved her off. "Don't give me that—he used a vile word—stuff!" He rose abruptly from his chair and added, "That theory—that interpretation—has been around for decades and I and my church don't believe in it."

Charlie didn't remember his mother's vernacular when it came to prophetic terms but he did know there were varied positions when it came to God and Jesus rescuing his Church from the judgments the prophets predicted would come upon the world. His mother believed that Jesus would never leave his bride, the name given to his church, behind during what his mother termed, the seven-year Tribulation period. *He had to know more.* "Hold on," he said, "let me check something out." With that he pulled out his cell phone and posted the question on the search engine: *What is the Rapture and the Tribulation?* Seconds later the answer appeared. He read it aloud:

"'The *Rapture* is an eschatological position noted in the Biblical text of First Thessalonians, that is held by some Christians, particularly those of American evangelicalism, consisting of an end-time event when all dead Christian believers will be resurrected and, joined with Christians who are still alive, together will rise 'in the clouds, to meet the Lord in the air—'"

He paused and glanced at pastor Ron who gave him a tired, cynical look. He continued in a voice sounding as if he were beginning to understand:

"'Every Christian that has ever existed throughout the course of the entire Christian era will be instantaneously transformed in a perfect resurrected body and will thus escape the trials of the Tribulation. Those who become Christians after the Rapture will live through (or perish during) the Tribulation. After the Tribulation, Christ will return to establish his Millennial Kingdom. The meaning of the word Rapture is found in the Greek to mean 'caught-up' or 'to seize,' and is held as being pre-dispensational, a view of futurism that considers various prophecies in the Bible as remaining unfilled and occurring in the future. Pretribulationism distinguishes the Rapture from the Second Coming of Jesus Christ. This view holds that the Rapture would precede the seven-year Tribulation, which would culminate in Christ's second coming on the Mount of Olives in Jerusalem and be followed by a thousand-year Messianic Kingdom. This interpretation supports the idea that a large segment of humanity will be left behind on earth for the seven-year judgment period described in the book of Revelation, the last book of the New Testament.'"

Pastor Ron walked in front of Charlie then glanced at Maureen while crossing his arms across his chest. "Do you believe this false interpretation? This baloney?"

"Well—" Charlie hesitated then: "It sounds true. I mean what else could be the explanation?"

Outraged at the idea, Pastor Ron spluttered, "You can't really buy into this stuff—because if you do—I have a question for you!"

"Okay," Charlie asked slightly bewildered. "What—?"

"If you really believe this nonsense about the *Rapture* and claim to be a Christian, why are you still here? Why didn't you go up with Jesus as well?" Pastor Ron asked defiantly.

"Hmm. I have to think about that for a moment," he said solemnly.

Maureen raised her hand to support Charlie. "Maybe we're not the—" she paused and made quotation marks in the air. "—'Christians' we thought we were."

"That may very well be," Charlie replied unpleasantly.

Pastor Ron swore vehemently then snarled, "What are you saying—that I'm not a Christian? That the people in my congregation are not Christians?"

"I really can't answer that," Maureen replied in an attempt to attenuate the agitation. "I must admit that I'm not a believer in the Bible and don't profess to be a Christian. I can't label myself an atheist because I do believe in some god, but I also believe there are many ways to get to heaven, Jesus being just one of them. So I can't offer an explanation." With that she shrugged her shoulders and looked to Charlie. "Charlie—?"

Charlie gave her a sidelong look she couldn't decipher then for a moment he busied himself scrolling through his cell phone for additional information relative to their debate. He halted his search on a Bible prophecy website and began to read it. Moments passed.

"Charlie?" Maureen gave him a warning frown as he appeared to take too long. "What's happening?" She could tell by his cryptic look that he was having trouble understanding or believing what he was reading. She realized he was meditating on the subject.

Silence.

"Aahhh! Charlie?" Pastor Ron skewered him a look. "Care to share?"

He held up his cell phone in the air and said, "I'm afraid you're not going to like what I'm about to say, but according to what I just read, we're really in for a rough time in the years to come.

"This commentary on Bible passages like Ezekiel thirty-eight and Matthew twenty-four give us an explanation of what is going to happen. It cites the Islamic-Russian-China alliance will invade Israel soon after the *Rapture* of the church. This evil coalition will be led by the Antichrist who will perform in the Jerusalem temple what is known as 'the Abomination of Desolation' cited by Jesus and Daniel the prophet. This Antichrist offers up a sacrifice proclaiming to be god."

"Um," Maureen uttered. "That evil alliance was all over yesterday's news—the formation of what Israel labeled the 'axis powers.' They're preparing for all-out war."

Pastor Ron shook his head as he suddenly remembered learning about eschatology when he was in seminary. But to him it was more like fables and science fiction than prophecy so he never believed it nor taught on it. He remembered reading Hal Lindsey's book, *The Late Great Planet Earth* with extreme prejudice and disbelief but there too, he dismissed it since many of his predictions were yet to materialize. To him the whole prophetic theme in the Bible was riddled with varied interpretations and commentary that was dependent on what denomination wrote it. So he avoided it. Now he sorely regretted that mindset.

He did an internal assessment and knew within himself that he needed help. He realized his inadequacy when it came to prophecy. He turned to Charlie. "What is your take on things? What do you suggest we do?"

"From what I gather by reading these commentaries together with what I remember from what my mom said . . . " he hesitated. " . . . only those who received Christ as their Savior went to heaven. Those who are left behind—and that includes us—are to go through the next seven years of divine calamities that will be increasingly more severe. They are called the Seal, Trumpet, and Bowl judgments."

Pastor Ron gestured angrily as if he should have known this prediction then grabbed his King James Bible off his desk and abruptly swiped the pages until he reached Revelation. He scanned the background text then turned to chapter nine [later he would realize why he chose that chapter since it describes the Trumpet judgments that takes place midway through the horrible Tribulation period. He thought that if he were to experience the judgments that they would lessen toward the end. But he was wrong]. "Ugh!" he said as his eyes bored into Charlie asking the question that he couldn't voice: *What do we do now?* "This text says, 'But the rest of mankind, who were not killed by these plagues, did not repent of the works of their hands, that they should not worship demons, and idols of gold . . . and they did not repent of their murders or their sorceries or their sexual immorality or their thefts.'"

"Yeah, the part where 'neither did they repent . . . ' is really heavy to say the least," Charlie noted. "In my mind that means that humanity will not heed God's warnings regarding sexual perversion—among other forms of sinful activities—and that they will worsen over the next seven years. There is no sign of repentance or of God's forgiveness since there is no confession of sin by mankind—"

BANG! BANG! BANG!

A deafening knocking on the door!

Pastor Ron rushed to the door just as it burst open. "WELL! WHAT THE HELL IS HAPPENING?!" a woman cried out with a faction of the church standing behind her.

"Rikki! What is going on with you!" Pastor Ron exclaimed. Then he turned to Charlie and Maureen and said calmly in an attempt to sooth the abrupt invasion, "This is my wife Rikki."

"The congregation is going crazy!" she glowered. "You're the pastor here, what are we to do?"

"We've been doing some research on this disaster and I'm afraid to make any definite statements," he ventured as he pointed to Maureen and Charlie, "but it seems like God is going to bring judgment on the world and has removed his believers—the real Christians—before it starts."

Rikki spun around and then shrugged her shoulders. "What do you mean 'his believers, the true Christians'?" Defiantly: "Aren't we 'his believers'?"

Maureen grabbed Charlie's phone as the tone of the conversation began to escalate into what would become a fever pitch. She carefully noted a cross reference to the Revelation text that cited a passage out of Matthew twenty-four and read the verse quickly to herself: " . . . many will be offended, will betray one another, and will hate one another . . . and lawlessness will abound . . . " She suddenly realized what was happening. Violence throughout the world was going to escalate and permeate the world and that included the corporate church. "We need to get out of here!" she bellowed as she clutched Charlie's hand.

Rikki and the rest of the group circled pastor Ron to demand a deeper explanation as Maureen and Charlie wiggled their way out of the office and then scooted into the parking lot.

Ten miles away from the Lakeview Christian Church they pulled into a supermarket parking lot to rest a while to meditate and digest the event. After serious contemplation Maureen turned to him and asked, "Do you . . . " she fumbled for words, "really believe all that stuff about the *Rapture* and the real Christians suddenly disappearing?"

Definitely worried and perplexed: "I'm not sure—"

Maureen nor Charlie would not be able to give their editor a clear and concise report about their journey to Cody when they returned. It would take several weeks for them to discern truth from fiction, and even then they were not sure.

DARKENED MOON

YERKES OBSERVATORY, WILLAMS BAY, WISCONSIN

*N*ighttime is my special time to view the sky, our solar system, and what lies beyond, astronomer Jesse Steinberg thought as he programed the 40-inch refractor telescope to view the Taurus-Littrow landing site where the Apollo-17 LEM excursion took place in 1972. This was the final landing where scientist-astronaut Harrison Schmitt set up the sixth automated research station and drove the lunar rover vehicle a total of 30.5 kilometers over the Moon's surface.

Steinberg loved being an astronomer and worked hard at achieving that title. It took him over ten years of advanced schooling in astrophysics to earn his PhD in Planetary Sciences from the University of Arizona and often looked with pride at his diplomas on the wall at his station at the observatory.

Yerkes Observatory had both reflective and refractive telescopes, but only the refractor would be used to view Earth's moon because of its close proximity to Earth. No, he couldn't see the American flag planted on the lunar surface, nor could any telescope on Earth view the flag for that matter, but he enjoyed observing Earth's satellite since it was the first lunar landing inaugurated by President Kennedy in 1969 when he was a teenager that initiated the driving force to be an astronomer.

But today's observation of the Moon would not be like any other day where he would study it. No today would be quite different.

"Humph," Steinberg said to himself as he looked at the Moon's north pole. "Now that's strange!" He noticed a shift in the axis. Normally it was about 1.5 degrees but now it was nearly 2.5, a significant difference. The normal axial tilt kept the moon from experiencing noticeable seasons and kept some areas from being lit by sunlight with other areas being in perpetual shadow. While it's true that the Moon keeps the same face to us, this only happens because the Moon rotates at the same rate as its orbital motion, a special case of tidal locking called synchronous rotation.

He carefully studied the Highlands area, the seas, and the craters near to where the Apollo astronauts landed and didn't notice any changes there, but the axial shift troubled him. Minutes later after he rechecked the calibration on the Moon's orbit around the Earth and realized it too had changed. "Not good," he whispered. The Moon was 3,000 miles closer to Earth and was 30 percent brighter. He thought it was a supermoon but that celestial event was not scheduled for another three months. *Perplexing*, he thought.

He knew that the pull of the Moon's gravity on the Earth holds our planet in place. Without the Moon stabilizing our tilt, it is possible that the Earth's orbital tilt could be erratic resulting in the absence of seasons and that extreme weather patterns could lead to another ice age. But before that occurs the change in the Moon's tilt could affect tidal movements along with nocturnal animal navigation and human sleep patterns. "No, this is not good," he repeated as he rechecked his historical logs. No, this had never happened before since the astronomical sciences had kept records. *No, this was scary.*

He paused temporarily to gather his thoughts and reckon with his interpretations. He had to summon the director.

Franklyn Persac was appointed observatory director at Yerkes five years ago and in Steinberg's mind was a well-qualified astronomer and astrophysicist with multiple scientific degrees and experience that included many years of service at Mount Palomar. At age sixty-six he was extremely competent being endowed with a brilliant mind with an IQ of 148, close to Einstein's IQ of 160.

"Please verify and validate my findings," Steinberg said to Persac as he stepped away from the refractor telescope he was monitoring. "Something very strange is occurring here today with our Moon."

Persac sat in the observer's chair and remained silent as he studied the Moon and adjusted the telescope while checking Steinberg's notes. After ten minutes he turned to Steinberg and said, "Call NASA's director , Lester

Mason, right away and have him report to us if there is any shift in our military and commercial satellites, especially those in low-earth orbit." He turned in the chair to face Steinberg and stared at him in helpless frustration. He shook his head and added, "This is serious.

"If our lunar orbit has changed it will have a catastrophic effect on us. The lunar cycle impacts human reproduction in fertility, menstruation, and birth rates. Tides are the result of the gravitational tug from the Moon and Sun that the Earth feels. Without our Moon the Earth's tilt could increase as high as forty-five degrees causing all life on Earth to perish. Our Moon makes Earth a livable planet by moderating our home's planet's wobble on its axis that leads to a stable climate. It causes tides, creating a rhythm that has guided humans for thousands of years."

Steinberg turned to leave and make the call to NASA when Persac grabbed hold of his arm. "Let me know what's happening the minute you get on the phone with him."

Steinberg got the message: things were very serious, even life-threatening for Earth.

* * *

The return call from NASA was quicker than expected. Steinberg grew thoughtful then picked up his desk phone, put it on speaker and said, "Good afternoon Dr. Mason. We're surprised to hear from you so soon after my call." He waved to director Persac for him to join him then added to Mason, "What's the latest on our request and your surveillance?"

"Hmm, well," he began somberly, "we have a problem—actually it's more than one. I checked our LEO's (Low Earth Orbit) satellites that are closest to Earth, and their orbits are decaying three times faster than normal. These satellites orbit up to 1,200 miles above the Earth on the same altitude as our International Space Station, the Hubble Telescope and some 4,000 Space X Starlink satellites.

"We're still in the process of calibrating our MEO's (Medium Earth Orbit) satellites that are used for navigation and GPS as well as our HEO (High Earth Orbit) satellites that are used for communication, remote sensing, and satellite radio.

"Based on our current findings there seems to be a radical orbital decay in everything close to Earth that includes the Moon and all the man-made stuff that is orbiting the Earth."

"Uh-oh!" Steinberg uttered while shaking his head then shot a look at Persac who looked perplexed—very perplexed.

"There's one more thing—" Mason said as he hesitated fractionally. "—we've noticed a change in the sun's distance from the Earth. Of course we know during the Earth's annual orbit around the sun that the distance changes accordingly, but we have records as to what the distance should be for this time of year and we see a big change." He cleared his throat. "We'll keep you updated as we check our low-and high-level orbiting satellites, but we need to hear from you and your astronomical observatory's network regarding the change of distances of both the Sun and Moon." Then he hung up the phone rather quickly without saying goodbye or good luck. His report and reaction bothered both Steinberg and Persac.

Steinberg's felt the hackles on his neck rise. He turned from his desk and slowly walked to the observatory's small kitchen, went to the coffee urn and poured himself a cup and despite his pledge to diet, grabbed a chocolate glazed donut, sat down at the table and pondered what just happened. When he glanced over at his desk he realized Persac was still at the telescope. He forgot all about him.

I need to go home early tonight, he promised himself. When he approached Persac to leave, Persac could recognize his astronomer's vexed countenance. "Go home," he said as the realization of events crashed in upon him. "Get some rest and we'll examine and try to discover what's causing these weird events tomorrow morning and if need be, we'll call in additional support. Come early."

Steinberg sighed deeply and nodded. "Thanks."

But the solution would not come tomorrow.

* * *

STEINBERG RESIDENCE, WILLAMS BAY, WISCONSIN

Being married to Jesse for over thirty years enabled his wife, Rebekah, to recognize something was wrong the moment he walked in their front door. It was written all over his face. Being 'empty-nesters,' she anxiously waited for his return every day and even had the coffee and his favorite treat ready for his arrival. *But today would be different.* "What's going on at work? You look like you saw a ghost or something," she asked as the tension worsened.

Steinberg kneaded his temples. "I need a glass of wine to calm me down," he said after giving her a warm embrace. As he sat down on a kitchen chair he added, "Our world is in trouble!"

He immediately transferred his anxiety to her. She smiled mirthlessly at him and said, "Okay, tell me what's going on."

He took a long sip of his wine and replied, "There's been a major shift in our solar system that I, and I'm sure there are other astronomers, recognized when I was viewing the Moon. There's orbital decay in our Sun, our Moon, and our orbiting satellites."

Rebekah nodded silently then walked to the kitchen sink to pour out her coffee cup then filled it up with wine. "What did Dr. Persac say about this?"

"Very troubled to say the least," Steinberg explained. "He immediately told me to contact NASA to confirm and within the hour they verified our findings—" he paused to take another long sip, "—so Persac advised that we take a break and try to make some sense of this in the morning. So he sent me home!"

Her anxiety heightened. "Wait a minute, wait a minute!" she shouted as her mind seized up on panic. "You're not going to believe this but I was watching some pastor of a big church this morning on TV and he was saying that the Bible predicts that the heavens will undergo huge changes as we near the time of Christ's return. In fact, he even mentioned that—" she paused to scratch her head, "—he even mentioned there would be a major change in the Sun and Moon."

Steinberg could feel her intensity charging the room. "I know we haven't been going to church in a few years, but can you call or signal one of the pastors from our church and ask him to come and explain to us what's going on?"

Rebekah took a long sip of coffee that turned to wine then replied assuredly, "I'll call him first thing in the morning."

Steinberg motioned for a refill then added, "Okay, I'm sure we'll all be fine once we find out this whole thing that happened is just a fluke and easily remedied."

"May that statement go from your mouth to God's ears," she said as fear iced through her.

But when Steinberg fell asleep after his two glasses of wine, Rebekah called their church to set up a meeting with one of their pastor's ASAP, telling them she believed a prophecy was coming true based on what her husband as an astronomer observed.

They were very interested.

* * *

At seven-thirty in the morning the Steinberg's doorbell rang. "Who could that be?" Steinberg asked as he finished getting dressed for the day.

"It's probable someone from the church," Rebekah replied. "I called them after you fell asleep and asked them to come over and talk to us about your report."

Steinberg shook his head several times. "I'm supposed to be at work early! I agreed to meet Persac," he argued.

Rebekah patted him on his shoulder. "He can wait! This is important!"

Moments later they were both at the front door. "Mr. and Mrs. Steinberg," the man began, "I'm pastor Errol Klein. I'm here in response to your phone call. It sounded urgent."

"It is urgent!" Steinberg replied and ushered him into their kitchen. "Come, sit down while we put up some coffee. We're very concerned about current events—" he paused then added, "—the current events taking place in the sky and our solar system, not on Earth!"

Pastor Klein nodded and pointed to Rebekah. "After I received your phone call I did some Online checking and truthfully there isn't much out there in the way of information, either on NASA or government websites. It's like there's a big shush!"

"I can understand that," Steinberg replied. "If this doesn't change, we're in for some real serious—" he paused momentarily, "—not serious, but catastrophic consequences, even doomsday."

Rebekah poured out the coffee, then asked pastor Klein, "What is the Biblical significance of all of this? I was watching TV and one of the popular evangelists quoted from the Bible something about what would come upon the Earth and the heavens before Jesus returns. Is that all true?"

Pastor Klein appeared to be in his 60s with graying hair and a black and white short-clipped beard augmented with blue jeans and a polo shirt. He looked very contemporary. But their concern was his Bible knowledge, not his looks. He reached into his jeans and pulled a pocket Bible and said softly as to allay any fears, "I often address Bible prophecy, but truthfully—"

he took a deep breath, "—I never thought I would live to see the day when it would come to pass while the church is still here."

Every word was like a whiplash to Steinberg. "What are you saying? Are we going to be here on planet Earth when God brings judgment? I thought—"

Pastor Klein waved him off. He understood his fears. "No, I don't mean that true Christians will be here during what the Bible calls the seven-year tribulation period, but I do believe—especially in view of current events—that we will see a glimpse of what is to come and recognize what we will be spared and use it as an opportunity to preach the Gospel. Then when things really begin to 'pop' we will be taken away in what is called the *Rapture* if we have a personal relationship with Jesus Christ."

"Whew! That's a relief," Rebekah exclaimed. But the issue of having a personal relationship with Christ disturbed her.

Seconds later Pastor Klein opened up his Bible and turned to the book of Joel. "I have a series of references that speak of the end times that I reviewed after hearing from Rebekah. Let me share some of them with you so we can figure out what's happening." *God may conceal the purpose of His ways, but his ways are not without purpose,* he thought. *Lord, help me to know your purpose.*

He put on his glasses to read the small print. "This is out of chapter two:

'The Earth quakes before them—'"

He paused and commented, "—the recent earthquake in Syria during the Islamic verses Israeli ongoing war is indicative of this, not to mention the great increase in quakes around the world." Then he continued:

> "'—the heavens tremble; the Sun and Moon grow dark, and the stars diminish their brightness . . . for the day of the Lord is great and very terrible; who can endure it? Now therefore, says the Lord, turn to Me with all your heart with fasting with weeping , and with mourning. So rend your heart, and not your garments; return to the Lord your God . . . and he will relent from doing harm. Who knows if He will turn and relent—?'"

Steinberg grabbed the Bible from Pastor Klein's hand. "Let me see that!" he cried out as he scanned the page. "This is really creepy! Are you saying that God predicted all this?"

"Nothing takes God by surprise," Pastor Klein replied. "As an omnipresent, omniscient, omnipotent God, this is all his doing!" He took his

Bible back and said, "And that's just the beginning. Now listen to the rest from Joel—and we haven't even gotten into other Old Testament prophets or the New Testament where Christ and Paul expand on these prophecies. Listen:

> "'And I will show wonders in the heavens and in the earth: Blood and fire and pillars of smoke. The Sun shall be turned into darkness, and the Moon into blood, before the coming of the great and awesome day of the Lord. And it shall come to pass that whoever calls on the name of the Lord shall be saved . . . the Sun and Moon will grow dark, and the stars will diminish their brightness—'"

Pastor Klein could read their faces. They were not only surprised with the prophecies but were fearful as well. "As an astronomer you have been given a preview of what's to come," he elaborated. "But most won't know until things really worsen, and even then, according to prophecy, they won't turn to the Lord but to their own devices to rid themselves of the ensuing physical and emotional pain. Very unfortunate."

It provided a modicum of satisfaction as far as Steinberg was concerned, but he had to get to work, he needed the release. He stood up and shook Pastor Klein's hand and said, "Thanks very much for coming and explaining things to us, but I have to get going." He glanced at his wristwatch. "My director is already waiting for me."

"I hope to see you at our church," Pastor Klein said and began to accompany Steinberg out of the house.

"Before you go," Rebekah said to the pastor, "I just want you to know that we really appreciated you taking the time to visit us and especially for your explanation of what's happening all around us. I hope to gain more of a better relationship with God before things really get dicey."

Pastor Klein shook her hand. "May that request go right to God's throne." Then he walked with Steinberg out of the house.

* * *

YERKES OBSERVATORY, WILLAMS BAY, WISCONSIN

"You're late!" Persac said the moment he spotted Steinberg coming in the observatory back door.

Steinberg did not have a wonderful morning nor did he want to upset the director. "Sorry, but my wife was so terrified about what's happening she called the pastor of our church who made an early morning visit to explain what the Bible has to say about this crisis."

Persac waved him off. He wasn't interested. "Mason from NASA called me at first light and gave me an update," he began, his tone displaying concern.

Steinberg stared blankly. "What did he say?"

After nervously scratching his head for a moment he replied, "Very alarming! He wanted us to confirm their calculations, but he said that the Moon appeared to be entering into a phrase of darkening that leads to what is called a 'blood Moon' that occurs when the Earth's Moon is in a total lunar eclipse."

Steinberg suddenly remembered Pastor Klein quoting from the book of Joel almost word for word what he just heard from Persac. "Ugh!" he gulped. "Anything else?"

"He added that the distances between Earth, the Sun, and Moon appeared to be changing," he said dolefully. "Yesterday, we both hoped it was a brief event, but apparently it is not. It's not going away! It's almost—" he struggled for words, "—it's almost as if some celestial spirits were giving us a message. I hope I can figure it out and warn the world . . . " he trailed off in deep meditation.

"Yeah! That's the operative phrase for the day, 'I hope I can figure it out.' But can we without looking to the God of our heavens?" Steinberg asked as the mystery escalated. He went into deep contemplation as well. ' . . . *before the coming of the great and awesome day of the Lord . . .* ' stuck in his mind. It wouldn't leave.

He had to call Rebekah.

"I'm at the church," Rebekah said on her cell phone. "The pastor called me and said that he was calling a church-wide prayer meeting and for me to join them." Overwhelmingly, "You should come!"

"But I'm at work—"

"Jesse, this is important," her voice fraught with tension.

His hands still tightly balled at his sides, he said, "I'll be right there!"

* * *

WILLIAMS BAY CHRISTIAN CHURCH

For a non-denominational church Steinberg was surprised there were so many cars in the parking lot. "Looks crowded," Persac said. *Rebekah is going to keel over when she sees Persac coming with me,* Steinberg thought to himself.

At the front door were two greeters. "Coming for the prayer meeting?" the teenager asked.

Steinberg nodded. "Where to?"

The teen beckoned for them to follow him. "This way gentlemen," he said and led them to the sanctuary.

Rebekah immediately spotted them above the crowd. Over here!" she shouted. Seconds later they met and she quickly recognized her husband's boss. "It's wonderful to see you Mr. Persac—" she paused, shook her head and added, "—I wish it were under more pleasant circumstances."

Persac bent in closer to her. "So do I," he complained just above a whisper.

Rebekah grabbed Steinberg's hand and pulled him aside. "What happened—how did you persuade him to come to a prayer meeting? Based on our knowledge of him being a 'super scientist' he's only one step above an atheist."

Steinberg shrugged his shoulders. "Believe me—it wasn't me. I think this whole catastrophe really scared the—" he used a vile word, "—out of him. So I think he's so frightened he—along with this whole church—is looking for answers and what to do."

"Can I have your attention?" Pastor Klein shouted out as the crowd began to settle down in the pews. "We need to identify the problem, then bring it before the heavenly throne of grace for God to help us," he noted in a slightly lower volume. Then he added, "I realize many of you are not part of our congregation—and that doesn't really matter, because we're all in this together. So let me open with prayer, then we'll read from the Bible to get some context, then we'll have a group prayer."

He prayed to the God of the Bible for guidance for several minutes, then he opened it up. "I'm reading from the book of Isaiah in the Old Testament, chapter thirteen.

> "'The Sun and Moon will grow dark, and the stars will diminish their brightness.'

"Now to Matthew twenty-four:

146

'Immediately after the tribulation of those days the Sun will be
darkened, and the Moon will not give its light, the stars will fall
from heaven, and the powers of the heavens will be shaken. Then
the sign of the Son of Man will appear in heaven. . .'"

He paused and explained. "A learned man by the name of Glasow
once said, 'One of the true tests of leadership is the ability to recognize a
problem before it becomes an emergency.' Well, I want to explain something to you. God has predicted what is happening so we can prepare
before it becomes an emergency.

"The events we are presently experiencing in our world and beyond—and I have the real scoop from one of our fellow Christians here
who is an astronomer over at Yerkes Observatory—is that our solar system, and probably beyond based on these verses we read, is undergoing a
calamitous change. This change that is described in these texts was prophesied thousands of years ago and their purpose is to announce the soon
return of Jesus Christ. The event is so magnificent that the whole universe
will applaud his appearance by undergoing a never-before metamorphous
into what the Bible refers to as the Millennial reign where Christ will
dwell on earth for one-thousand years—" he paused and explained, "—if
you want more info on this subject, come see me or one of our deacons
after this prayer meeting.

"But for now, suffice to say that God is going to get the world's attention to alert them to his presence—no He's not sleeping—and his presence
will be clear as these prophecies progress to their final fulfillment. The
triggering mechanism is seen in our current events where our world has
turned away from believing in the God of the Bible and replaced it with
humanism, materialism, hedonism, and every other 'ism' you can think of
and the God of heaven has now said, 'It's enough!' Then add to this all the
enemies of Israel rearing their ugly heads and then you see that the time
is right for God to act—"

"PASTOR, LOOK OUTSIDE!" Someone from the pews shouted out.

The whole church immediately grew restless and noisy as Pastor
Klein turned and stared out the upper windows then checked his wristwatch. It was only 3:15 P.M. but it was beginning to get dark and there
were no clouds to block the sun. He remembered the Biblical text and the
spirit inside him would not allow him to hold it in. He had to announce
it. "Listen up!" he shouted out. "I want to show you how important these

days are in view of prophecy." He opened his Bible to the book of Revelation and turned to chapter eight. "Here this:

> 'Then the fourth angel sounded and a third of the Sun was struck, a third of the Moon, and a third of the stars, so that a third of them were darkened. A third of the day did not shine, and likewise the night—'"

He paused and exclaimed after biting his lower lip, "We are experiencing the beginning of this today!" He nodded to his deacons then extended his arms outward toward the congregation and said with brightening eyes, "If anyone does not have a personal relationship with Jesus Christ, let them come forward and pray with us right now so you can be saved and spared from the wrath to come!"

When Persac heard the pastor's explanation fear overcame him. He began breathing in ragged gasps. He turned to Steinberg. "What should we do?"

Steinberg signaled Rebekah to join him then said, "I know what to do." Then he clutched Persac's hand and walked to Pastor Klein standing in front of the pulpit. "We want that!" Steinberg said to him with tearful eyes. More than twenty-five came forward for the invitation to receive Jesus as their Savior.

It would be another hour before the whole congregation would unite as one in prayer.

AUTHOR'S PROFILE

Doctor Curtin, originally from Long Island, New York, relocated in South Florida in 1987 to direct a large Christian ministry with its focus on Jewish evangelism. Within three years he resumed his ministerial studies, earning a B.S. and M.A. in Biblical Studies from Trinity Evangelical Divinity School in Deerfield, Illinois. From there he went on to earn a Doctor of Ministry degree in Christian Counseling from the South Florida Bible College and Theological Seminary in Deerfield Beach, Florida, where he presided as Academic Dean and professor of Biblical Studies. Dr. Curtin is presently an adjunct professor for Trinity College in Deerfield, IL as well as a pastor emeritus in a large denominational church in Florida. He and his helpmate of over sixty years, Kathy, have two children, seven grandchildren, and one son who is now with the Lord in glory.

His first work of prophetic fiction, *The Agenda*, published as one of six books in the Tribulation Series by Wipf & Stock chronicles the rise of the Antichrist through the discovery of the AIDS vaccine. This book was followed up by the sequel, *The Lights of God* that dramatizes the modern discovery of the ancient Biblical revelatory device used by the Hebrew high priest, the Urim and Thummim, and its role in the exposure of the Antichrist. The third book in the futuristic series, *The Seven Seals*, portrays life during the initial period of the Tribulation. The fourth book, *The Seven Trumpets* was followed by the final book in that series, *The Seven Bowls*. All of these are dramatic views of the last years of the Great Tribulation period predicted by Christ in Matthew chapter 24. The Family Matter, a novel that addresses the plight of America's homeless and the call of the Christian Church to minister to them, was reprinted by Wipf and Stock along with *The Family Secret*.

The idea to write biblical fiction goes back many years; long before The Left Behind series became popular. Unfortunately, his name was not as well known, so the prophetic fiction novel he wrote took a long time to be recognized. Many of the characters are composites of people in his life, while others are pure literary invention. His passion to write prophetic fiction emerged from his love for the Bible and its view toward the future. Remarkably, current events continue to intrigue him as he sees the fulfillment of the very prophecies God predicted. *The Vaccine* is a current example of the events foretold in Bible prophecy. Therefore, his writing takes on more of an admonition than just a fictional story. His desire to write contemporary fiction emerged from his observation of society's needs as he saw them. Meeting the needs of the hurting in our world is an obligation he believes should be met by those who are able, whether they are in the world or in the church.

Emerging from his ministry as the Senior Pastor of a church in So. Florida that hosts both a Brazilian and Haitian group is a church life book entitled, *Sharing Your Church Building*. This non-fiction book is currently a reprint of Wipf & Stock Publishing and will prove to be a valuable tool in the hands of the pastor experiencing the blessing of hosting divergent ministries under one banner in the Christian Church. His second non-fiction reprinted book entitled *Waking the Sleeping Church* is designed to provoke the Christian Church to action amidst the ongoing deterioration of values in our nation and the Church's calling to be a light in a darkening nation. Wipf & Stock published his third non-fiction book, *Monuments*, in 2020. This book, *Short Stories for the Christian Life* is his latest endeavor to minister to the corporate church through snapshots of life as a Christian.